### "I WANT THAT KISS. AND I INTEND TO TAKE IT!"

Not roughly, but almost reverently, his fingers closed on a handful of silken tresses. Then he looked into her gray eyes, so wide, so apprehensive, so luminous in the light that filtered through the screen. She felt the small tongues of fire that leaped high and higher, touching her, warming her, willing her to come to him. His head bowed, and just before she closed her eyes she saw his lips part—firm, hot, moist, as they came toward hers. Demanding—not asking! They seduced her senses, leaving her awash with unwilling desire. . . .

## A CANDLELIGHT ECSTASY ROMANCE ®

# BY PASSION BOUND

*Emma Bennett*

*A CANDLELIGHT ECSTASY ROMANCE* ®

Published by
Dell Publishing Co., Inc.
1 Dag Hammarskjold Plaza
New York, New York 10017

Dell ® TM 681510, Dell Publishing Co., Inc.

Candlelight Ecstasy Romance®, 1,203,540, is a registered
trademark of Dell Publishing Co., Inc., New York, New
York.

ISBN: 0–440–10918–3

Printed in the United States of America

First printing—April 1983

To Our Readers:

We have been delighted with your enthusiastic response to Candlelight Ecstasy Romances®, and we thank you for the interest you have shown in this exciting series.

In the upcoming months we will continue to present the distinctive sensuous love stories you have come to expect only from Ecstasy. We look forward to bringing you many more books from your favorite authors and also the very finest work from new authors of contemporary romantic fiction.

As always, we are striving to present the unique absorbing love stories that you enjoy most—books that are more than ordinary romance.

Your suggestions and comments are always welcome. Please write to us at the address below.

Sincerely,

The Editors
Candlelight Romances
1 Dag Hammarskjold Plaza
New York, New York 10017

# CHAPTER ONE

It was early evening when Megan pulled up in front of the deserted old frame house, but because of daylight savings time, the sun was still shining. Her eyes, a soft, warm gray, reflected a reserved and distant look, and her dark brown hair, pulled back from her face in a ponytail, accented the exhaustion mirrored in her features. She leaned over the steering wheel, her shoulders hunched, bowed as if she were carrying the weight of the world on them. Switching off the ignition, she sat for a while longer, not really wanting to move but knowing that she had to.

"Well, Bismarck," she said finally, addressing the black and tan German shepherd who slept on the back seat, "here we are."

Bismarck thumped his tail against the seat and whimpered lowly, acknowledging her words, but he didn't move until she opened his door. Then he sprang from the car to begin a careful investigation of the yard, smelling every bush and blade of grass in sight, intrigued with the south Texas backwoods.

Megan slung her purse over her shoulder and pulled her suitcase from the back seat. She carefully picked her way across the lawn, trudging up the three steps onto the wooden porch that extended across the entire front of the house. She dropped the suitcase and fished through her purse for the lone house key.

She was tired, she thought, and she should be. She had been driving nonstop all day, quickly marking the miles between Dallas and Los Nogalitos, a small community just east of Del Rio. She was happy that her grandfather had bought this old house so many years ago, and she was glad that she could come here now. His departure for Mexico had been a blessing, allowing Megan the time she needed to be by herself and think. To hide away and lick her wounds.

She walked through the living room into the front bedroom, carelessly throwing her suitcase on the bed. She then made her way to the kitchen where she filled the kettle with water and set it on the stove. While she waited for the water to boil, she rummaged through the refrigerator. Not much in the line of food, she thought, but enough for tonight and tomorrow. Monday she'd go into town for supplies.

By the time she had completed her inspection of the pantry and the cabinets, her coffee was ready, and she poured herself a cup, carrying it into the bedroom with her. As she drank it she unpacked the few clothes she had chosen to bring with her, hanging her skirt and blouse in the closet and arranging her underwear, shirts, and jeans in the dresser drawers. She walked into the large bathroom that was situated between the two bedrooms and turned the spigots on full force, filling the four-legged tub with water and a sudsy bubble bath. She stripped and climbed into the foamy water, hoping to soak away some of her weariness and misery.

When she was through bathing and shampooing her hair, she dried off and dressed in a pair of shorts and a cotton knit shirt. Then she quickly dried her hair and brushed it until it shone, letting it softly wave around her face. After she slipped into a pair of leather thongs, she padded into the kitchen to get another cup of coffee, thinking she might possibly open a can of something for supper, but she'd relax with her coffee first.

Afterward she decided to take Bismarck for a walk before the sun went down. Giving the gentle command, Megan led the way and the dog followed, soon losing himself in the grassland and racing with Megan. About an hour later a tired, panting Megan ran up the back steps into the kitchen, followed by Bismarck.

"I think it's time I consider my stomach," she told him fondly as she puttered around in the kitchen. "I thought to bring your food"—she leaned over to pour him a dishful of the bagged dog food—"but I've got to rustle mine up from somewhere."

She opened the pantry, rummaging until she found a can of soup and a tin box of crackers. She wasn't worried about the soup, but she hoped the crackers were still crisp. Still, beggars can't be choosers! She set them on the counter and knelt down to search for a pot, when Bismarck suddenly tensed, cocked his head, and darted into the living room, growling low in the back of his throat, his neck fur bristling.

Not one easily frightened, but one to be careful, Megan followed Bismarck into the room, moving toward the gossamer curtains, pulling them aside. She could see the pickup that was parked next to her car, and she could see a strange man angrily striding across the lawn. She heard the firm steps as they hit the porch, and she dropped the curtain, moving toward the door herself.

As her hand closed over the knob she expected to hear the knock, but instead the door was swept open with such force that she stumbled backward, falling against the back of the sofa.

11

"Who the hell are you, and what do you think you're doing in this house?"

The words were curt and abrasive, and the man was angry, very angry. His face was a mask of fury; his emerald green eyes were flares of rage.

Bismarck hunched between Megan and the man, snarling softly, his teeth bared, waiting for the command. The green eyes flitted over the dog, coming back to rest derisively on the woman.

In one hand he held his Stetson; the other tightly clung to the door. His rust-brown hair was ruffled and tossed by the evening breeze, and his eyes mirrored surprise, among other emotions. A spark of mockery seemed to dance there, too, in the golden lights that spiraled from the green depths.

"I asked you a question," he repeated. "I'd like to have an answer." His words were softly spoken, but laced with steel.

"I'd like to know why you barged into my house without knocking?" Megan returned coolly, not allowing herself to be intimidated by his height or his size.

"Your house," he spat. "What do you mean, your house?"

Still she didn't answer, and his eyes slowly traveled the length of her body, gazing at the soft swell of her breasts beneath the clinging cotton of her shirt, moving over the flat plane of her stomach to the long slim length of tanned legs that extended from her white shorts.

"Last I heard, this house belonged to Joel Leighton."

Megan, disliking the thick sarcasm in his voice, put more distance between them, not stopping until she hit the doorframe behind her. She didn't care much for his tone or, for that matter, his blatant appraisal.

"Last I heard," she mimicked, "Joel Leighton didn't need a keeper. Why don't you walk out, close the door behind you, and tend to your own business, cowboy?"

This time his eyes slowly, derisively, stripped her body of clothing piece by piece. Not to be outdone, she stood proudly, her back straight, her face calm, eyeing him with the same disdain.

"From the way you're gaping, cowboy, I'd say you've never seen a woman before."

Her gray eyes raked over him: the wind-tossed hair, the checkered shirt that caressed the broad shoulders and muscle-corded biceps, the muscular legs that fit snugly into a pair of faded jeans, the worn boots. She watched him impatiently slap his hat against one of his legs. She smiled, cool and distant, trying to compose her inward quaking.

Then her gray eyes, metallic sharp, traveled upward, and she was in charge. Her hand rested on Bismarck's head, and her fingers lightly stroked the bristled fur around his neck and face. The soft snarl could still be heard, and he was watching the stranger's every move.

"Oh, I've seen plenty of women before," he corrected her, "but I've never seen one of *Joel's* before."

Megan's smile was brittle and cold. Joel's woman! This man was not to be *believed*. "Wrong again. I'm not Joel's woman, as you so quaintly put it. And even if I were, I don't enjoy being referred to as if I were a piece of live-stock, cowboy."

She made no attempt to hide her irritation. In all her twenty-five years she had never been in a position like this one, nor had she ever met a man as obstinate and rude as this one. He was tough and hard; he was primitive. Yes, that was the word for him, she thought, primitive.

His eyes, now a deep hunter green, were glassy and hard, yet they perused her as if he were memorizing every detail of her appearance.

No smile; just a tightening of those chiseled, hard features; the green eyes deepening with threatening menace. He took another cautious step into the room, looking

13

warily at the dog. He spoke in a grating tone, his voice gravelly with anger. His hand balled into a fist, clenched tightly to his side.

"Who are you, and what are you doing here?"

Megan knew she could push him no further. He was livid with anger, as was she, but at the same time she was more frightened than he. Her imagination began to run wild. What if he had a gun? It would be a simple task to kill both her and Bismarck. Perhaps she'd better answer his question.

"Megan," she snapped irascibly. "Megan Jonas, Joel's granddaughter."

The only thing that moved on his body were those eyes—those green eyes. They slowly raked over her one more time before they stopped at her face, before he grinned. Then he softly laughed, his eyes, like the forest in early spring, green and warm, frolicking with gentle amusement. His lips curved into a sensuous smile. Throwing his hat on the sofa, he spoke again.

"My mistake, Megan Jonas, Joel Leighton's granddaughter."

Megan's anger was no longer at abeyance; she saw nothing funny about the scene at all, and her words effectively conveyed her rage. "Who are you?"

His eyes, no longer frosty and cold, caught and held hers, denying her the privilege of anger. But she refused to be conned by their beauty. She refused to be mesmerized by their charm.

"Are you going to tell me who you are?"

Fully cognizant of her anger, still laughing at her, he drawled in mimickery of the western vernacular, "Yes'm." He paused and drew a deep breath. "I'm Alan McDonald, Joel's nearest neighbor, who isn't so near."

"Aren't you rather presumptuous with someone else's property?" Megan inquired.

His brows rose, and his eyes clouded with question.

"Aren't you presumptuous in coming here without alerting someone first?"

"Why should I alert anyone?" she countered icily. "This happens to be my property as much as it's Gramps's!"

His eyes slowly, very slowly, moved across each feature of her face, the gray eyes defiant in spite of her fear, the outward veneer of self-confidence a calmness that would have fooled many. A calmness which would have intimidated many he thought with an inward smile.

"I wasn't aware that it was yours," he responded in a voice that was low but wasn't a whisper.

Megan grinned. "That proves my point, cowboy. You're pretty damn presumptuous."

Now his glance rested on the dog. "Not presumptuous, just responsible, Miss Jonas. Your grandfather did leave his property—" His thick lashes swept up, and his green eyes mocked her. "My mistake," he corrected himself, "your property, in my care."

"Really." Megan breathed sarcastically.

He shrugged. "Believe what you will, I don't care." Now his eyes swept around the room, taking in the clutter of its absent owner. "Why do you think Joel would go off to Mexico and leave his utilities on if I weren't here to look after things?"

Now it was Megan's turn to shrug, but he wasn't paying her any attention. He was kneeling down in front of Bismarck, tentatively holding out his hand. Bismarck, however, didn't accept the stranger's offer of friendship. But he did stop his growling, and his fur flattened against his sleek, well-proportioned frame.

Alan stood, slapping his hands lightly against the sides of his pants. "I'm sorry if I seemed abrupt, but I was worried when I drove by and saw the car. This is an ideal set-up for poachers." He looked at her. "Have you been here long?"

"Long enough," came Megan's curt answer. He had dallied with her too much, and she wasn't going to easily surrender to his sudden friendly overtures.

His russet brows cocked questioningly. "Haven't eaten yet?" She shook her head. "I thought so," he continued. "That explains why you're in such a foul mood."

"Food has nothing to do with my foul mood," she slashed, her eyes daggers of enmity and anger. "You are the reason for my foul mood. Before you came storming through the door I was about to prepare my supper."

He chuckled, unabashed by her accusation. "If I know Joel Leighton very well, he's more interested in his painting than his eating, so his cupboard's probably bare. You'll be doing pretty good to find enough to eat on until Monday."

"I'll manage." He couldn't fail to notice the dismissive tones.

She wanted no help from this man. In fact, the farther away he was, the better she would like it. She had driven down here to be by herself, and the last thing she wanted was company. She certainly didn't want his.

"I'll find enough, I'm sure," she reinforced caustically. "I'm only going to be here for a few days, and I'm quite able to take care of myself."

"You might be in the big city, ma'am," he drawled slowly, "but you're out of your environment now. Better let people help if they will."

He stepped toward the door, pushing on the screen. He had met and had known many women during his life, but Megan Jonas was refreshingly different. Despite all that outward gruffness and hostility, she was a person whom he wanted to know better, perhaps to know intimately.

"Look, cowboy," Megan snapped, "I'll take care of myself."

She didn't like him, he thought, sprinting down the steps. But that didn't bother him. If anything, it spurred his interest. At least it would give him a challenge. How long would it take for him to wear her resistance down? He almost chuckled, thinking of what her outburst would be if she could read his thoughts.

"I've got some groceries in the truck. Let's see what I can do."

"I said no thanks," Megan curtly replied, running across the room, pushing on the screen door. "I can manage by myself. I don't need your groceries."

"Sure you do," he replied over his shoulder with patient amusement, lifting two bags from the truck. He easily cradled them in the crook of each arm. "I've got plenty here, and there's no reason why we shouldn't share. That's what neighbors are for."

Megan groaned disgustedly, knowing that she had lost this round, but she argued no more. Rather, she opened the door, holding it until he had passed through. Then she followed him into the kitchen with Bismarck right at her heels.

"Put them on the table, and I'll put them away later."

Alan set them on the table, and although he heard that subtle command in her tone, he was in no hurry to leave. He turned, dropped his hands to his hips, and gazed around the small kitchen, his eyes stopping at the stove.

"Hmmm," he sniffed appreciatively, "that coffee smells good. May I have a cup?"

As personnel manager of Zelco Corporation in Dallas, Megan had learned to present a pleasant face and greeting at all times, but this was more than she could tolerate. Her dislike and animosity for Alan McDonald overruled her training and personal discipline.

"Look," she spat ungraciously, "I'm really very tired, and I'd like for you to leave so I can go to bed."

"Just one cup." The lopsided grin was her undoing.

"One cup," she acquiesced with a heavy sigh, "and then

17

it's home for you." She yanked on the cabinet door, grabbed a cup, and filled it.

"Thanks." His fingers curled around the large white mug.

"Think nothing of it, cowboy," she returned churlishly.

He placed one hand on the counter, palm down, and stared at her for endless seconds, holding his cup in the other hand. *All right, Megan Jonas,* he thought. *We'll play this hand the way you're dealing.* A grin—a full grin—curved those lips and gleamed in those emerald eyes.

"No, Miss Jonas." There was a mimicked slur on her name. "I'm not a cowboy."

Megan's brows rose, and she eyed him skeptically. He lifted the mug to his lips and drank, studying her over the rim. Her eyes could be beautiful, he thought. Should be a soft, gentle gray about the color of dove down, but they weren't now. They were a hard, steely gray, reminding him of a rapier. *On guard! She's sizing me up, getting ready for the attack.* It was all he could do to keep the laughter from bubbling over.

"Not everybody who lives out here is a cowboy, you know."

She didn't return his smile; their senses of humor were evidently very different. "No?"

"I'm a farmer . . ." His words were firm and sure, a certain pride underscoring them. "A dairy farmer." He set his mug on the counter and picked up the forgotten can of soup. He whirled it around in his hand, reading the label. Then he looked at Megan, devilish imps of humor leaping in his eyes. But he made no derogatory remarks. He just set the can down and moved to the table.

"Do you suppose that a girl fresh from the big city could cook a good wholesome meal for a hard-working farmer?"

"How do you know that I'm from the city?" she parried, refusing to answer his question.

"Lucky guess and picking up bits and pieces from what your grandfather said."

"If that's true, why did you put me through the first degree?"

"I didn't know you," he replied easily. "And from what Joel had said, I sorta expected a much younger granddaughter. You know, a ten- or eleven-year-old. I certainly didn't expect a woman."

Megan nodded. That sounded like Gramps, who refused to believe that she had grown up. And it was just like him not to have photos at the summer house.

"I said, can you cook?" he repeated.

"Maybe," she evaded. "Why?"

The paper bag crackled as his hands rummaged around inside it. "Because, ma'am, I have two steaks, some Irish potatoes, and lettuce and tomatoes." As he named each item, he laid it on the table. Then he lifted a bottle from the sack, smiling broadly. "And to top off the meal, this bottle of wine."

Megan shook her head and turned, opening the cabinet door again. "The food's fine," she said over her shoulder, "but can you imagine the incongruity of the wine and this?" She turned, holding an empty glass in front of herself.

He blinked his eyes blankly for a second, staring at her and the glass. "What incongruity?" he asked.

"Wine in a jelly glass?" she softly laughed, the sound musically warm and rich. "I think perhaps, Farmer McDonald, that I'll stick to iced tea."

He shrugged, his eyes twinkling. "Whatever. But I still think it's a good idea." His hand swept over the food that was lying on the table. "If you're willing to cook this, I'm willing to share it with you . . . and help you eat it."

Megan poured herself another cup of coffee; it helped alleviate the nervous tension that his nearness seemed to generate. She nodded her head and began to hum. Then she began to laugh to herself as she softly sang, "Old McDonald had a farm, Ee-i, ee-i, oh."

*She does have a sense of humor,* he thought, his eyes dancing to the tune. He nodded. "That's right. Old McDonald's Dairy Farm."

She sputtered, almost spitting out her swallow of coffee, then gulped it down quickly. "You mean—"

"I mean—" He chuckled.

"It certainly lacks for originality," she quipped sharply, flinching when her joke slapped her in the face.

Those lips curved upward, and victory glowed in his eyes. "Maybe it does lack for originality, but the name seemed to fit." He moved to the table, sat down, and looked up, again catching and holding captive gray eyes with his green ones. "I don't think I like the idea of your staying here by yourself, and I certainly don't think Joel would if he knew about it."

"What you think doesn't matter as much as a hill of beans," Megan retorted, tired of people's kindly advice on running her life. "And you have no idea whether Joel knows that I'm here or not."

"He doesn't," came the swift rejoinder. "If he had known, he would have made sure that you had plenty of groceries and supplies. If he had known," he went on relentlessly, "he would have been here waiting for you rather than tromping through Mexico."

"Maybe." She picked up the lettuce and tomatoes from the table and laid them in the sink, turning on the faucet, letting the water run over them. "However, as you've already observed, I'm hardly a little girl in need of Joel's watchful eye." She spun around. "And I'm quite capable of taking care of myself."

"Are you?" he murmured quietly, eyeing her with interest, seemingly able to see beyond that facade of sophistication and poise, finding the floundering little girl who was hiding behind it.

"Besides," she added, "I have Bismarck, and I'm not afraid with him."

"You may get more than you bargained for, Megan. What if I hadn't been a friendly neighbor?"

"Bismarck would have torn you to bits," she replied matter-of-factly.

She was tired of the endless sermons she had listened to in the past eight months, advice on how to mend a broken heart, counsel for the heartbroken, rules for surviving, ways to forget one man and to go about falling in love again. And if this country yokel started in, she thought, she would scream. She just wanted to be left alone to solve her problems by herself.

"I doubt that." The words were derisive and full of disdain and unbelief. His brows rose slightly, and his lips quirked in an incipient smile.

"Look, Mr. McDonald," Megan began, turning, wiping her wet hands on a dish towel, "I know you're trying to be helpful and neighborly." Her words were emphatically soft. "But I didn't invite you in, and I don't want you to stay. And I'm certainly not in need of your wisdom."

"How clarion can one get," Alan mocked with solemnity, his eyes narrowed and hooded by the thick russet lashes. "But I agree with you," he continued. "You are old enough to take care of yourself. I just wonder why you're not doing it."

Megan's temper got the best of her, and anger controlled her actions. She stamped her foot on the floor and blurted out, "Take your food—" She stopped talking, wheeled around, fumbled in the sink, lifting the lettuce and tomatoes. She handed the dripping vegetables to him. "Take these and get out. I came here to be by myself, and I don't want company anyway, much less yours."

Alan made no move to take the vegetables from her, nor did her heated outburst seem to daunt him. "Still, Miss Jonas"—the dripping water tapped as it splattered on the

21

floor and his boots—"you must know that it's foolish of you to stay here by yourself. If you weren't aware of that, you wouldn't be so upset by my pointing it out to you." He pointed to the floor. "You're dripping water with those. Why don't you put them back into the sink and go ahead and fix our dinner?"

If she hadn't felt so ridiculous and if she hadn't been so hungry, she would have thrown him out with his food right behind him. But as it was she laid the lettuce and tomatoes in the sink and began to put the rest of the staples away. With indolent ease, Alan leaned back in the chair, folding his hands behind his head, watching her. After a leisurely second cup of coffee, he spoke again.

"You wouldn't consider coming to stay with me, would you?"

Megan had never turned around so fast in her life. She almost dropped the canned goods, so great was her shock. Her face was stamped with that numbness that comes with incredulity, and her eyes were wide with shocked blankness.

"What?" She meant to sound reproving; however, the sound that came out was more like a shriek.

He laughed, the sound rich and mellow, a deep rumble coming from the broad expanse of his chest. "It's not what you're thinking and not what you'll probably have the right to think in the future," he promised her devilishly. "I'm thinking of your safety and Joel's peace of mind right now."

She set the cans on the shelf. "Pardon me," she purred sarcastically, "if I don't believe you." She slapped her hands together, wiping the dust off them. "But, at the risk of boring you, I will repeat myself. I'll take care of my own safety and the peace of my mind." She straightened the cans in the pantry, adding as an afterthought, "And I'll take care of my own body." Bismarck, hearing the harshness in her words, tensed, his eyes glued to Alan, his ears twitching slightly. Megan pointed to the door again for about the third time in one evening. "Please, leave. I'm too tired to engage in these senseless debates with you, tonight, Farmer McDonald. Perhaps some other time."

The smile was wiped from his eyes; however, his lips were still curved upward. Megan Jonas wasn't the sweet, unassuming little kitten that Joel had painted, Alan thought. She's a hellcat, bent on tasting blood. *And if I'm not careful,* he surmised, *it'll be my blood she's after. One bad experience and she's scarred for life.*

"Believe it or not, Megan," he said, slowly enunciating his words, his anger clearly under control, "I'm not interested in your virtue at the moment, although you do present a most alluring picture in your shorts and that clinging shirt." Megan gasped, but he continued to speak. "I happen to have a very respectable housekeeper who lives with me and is like a second mother to me. In fact, she's old enough to be my mother, and she's very circumspect and old-fashioned. If I had designs on your chastity, she would present an insurmountable obstacle."

"No," Megan returned, breathing deeply and heavily, still infuriated with his proposal. "No, thanks." She laughed dryly. "I've had offers before, but this one takes the cake. I guess it's the way of the backwoodsman." The flashing in the emerald eyes should have warned her, but it didn't. She was too caught up in her anger to notice him. She opened her mouth to vent some more of her ire when Alan stood up, moving steadily toward her.

"Look," he said softly, the words firmly undergirded with steel. "I'm tired of your insinuations and your insults. I've explained my purpose in asking you to stay at my house. You can take it or leave it. I don't care. If I wanted to make love to you, I'd just take you in my arms—" He took several more steps toward her, having reckoned on her reaction but not having reckoned on Bismarck's.

In that split second Megan softly called the dog's name, and he jumped to his feet, firmly planting himself between her and Alan, his teeth once again bared, snarling softly, tensed for the assault.

"And if I didn't want you to make love to me, Alan McDonald," Megan hissed between clenched teeth, "this is what I would do. Most find that Bismarck is a formidable foe. Also, Mr. McDonald, Bismarck understands my commands very well, and he reacts accordingly. Perhaps in the future you should consider this." She chuckled. "Bismarck is rather particular about who holds me."

Alan's eyes were narrowed, a wary speculativeness in the green depths. "My mistake, Megan. I should have reckoned on the big brute, but I didn't. I see that in order to get the beauty, I must learn to handle the beast."

"Friends or not," Megan warned him, "only I handle Bismarck. He's my dog, and no one else's."

That grin touched his lips again. "Then, my dear, I have only one recourse. I must learn to handle you." He laughed, and Megan bristled.

"Never," she spat. "You men are all alike—egotistical and selfish, just interested in what they can get out of the relationship, never giving any thought to the woman. Just interested in the handling."

"Tread softly, Meggie," Alan warned her, the flames of desire fanning readily in those green eyes. "I'm getting thoroughly intoxicated with the idea of manhandling you, if you know what I mean."

"This is my house, Mr. McDonald, and you are an uninvited guest. I would suggest that you control your tongue, even if you can't your mind, or get out. Since it's my house, I can't get angry and walk out, and since you're already inside, I can't slam the door in your face, so I'm telling you to stop giving me advice on how to live or how to love."

Alan grinned, totally unrepentant. "Okay, Megan, I'll

24

strike a compromise with you. If I don't give you any more advice or lessons, will you sheath your claws and have dinner with me?"

Megan shook her head irritably, trying to suppress the grin that was determined to surface. "You provide the food, and I cook?"

He nodded his head. "That's been the custom for thousands of years," he said. "Man provides the food; woman cooks. Also," he added, "no more of this miss or mister stuff, okay?"

The grin surfaced. "Okay," she agreed. "How about Farmer?"

He shook his head. "No, my name's not Farmer. I'm Alan. Say it."

Suddenly she felt gauche and schoolgirlish. She shrugged self-consciously. "I'll say it the next time I address you."

"Say it now," he enjoined firmly. "I want to hear you say my name."

"Alan," she replied, almost stumbling over it. "Alan McDonald."

"Wasn't so bad, was it?" He laughed. "I think it's a rather nice name. Most women do, you know?"

"I'm not most women," Megan informed him seriously.

All frivolity was erased from his face. "I'm as much aware of that as you are," he returned, his eyes riveting to hers. And she was surprised at what she saw. There was a tenderness and a gentleness hidden away in the deep recesses of those eyes, and they seemed to be for her—just for her. Quickly she dropped her eyes and turned around, making a pretense of beginning the meal.

He smiled. Megan had read his message. She hadn't responded, but she knew. "While you're cooking, I'll check to see that everything's locked up." He stopped in the door. "Do you know how to use a gun?"

"Good enough."

"Okay," he nodded. "I'll check to see that they're loaded."

After he left, Megan picked up his mug from the table and began to prepare dinner. She liberally seasoned the steaks and put them under the broiler. Then she peeled and sliced the potatoes for french fries, heating the grease in the iron skillet. While these were frying, she diced the tomatoes and cut the lettuce, making a tossed salad. Now for the tea.

Just as she set the pitcher on the table, Alan returned. "Mmmm," he sniffed, "smelling good already. I'm hungry."

"Me too," Megan admitted, pulling open the broiler door to check on the steaks. "I didn't realize how much so until I began to smell the food."

"What are you doing out here this time of the year?" Alan asked, pulling his chair out and sitting down again.

"Vacation," she replied, throwing the thick pot holder on the drainboard.

"First time you've been this way in a long time," he said casually, watching her intently as she answered.

"I was thinking about that earlier," she replied. "I haven't been here since I graduated from high school."

"Which was?" She noticed the definite twinkle in his eyes.

"Are you asking me how old I am?"

"I am, Megan Jonas." Soft laughter accompanied the words.

She laughed with him. "I'm twenty-five, and I haven't been here in about seven years." She questioned him. "How old are you?"

Tongue-in-cheek, he said, "I believe sagacious old men are ageless."

Megan grinned, undaunted. "But you're not ageless. You look as if you've been around for a while."

"Below the belt, Meggie," he admitted with a grin. "I'm thirty-three."

"And how long have you been living out here? I don't remember your being here when I used to come with Gramps."

"I haven't been here that long. About four years. Now the next question is mine. Why haven't you been here in so many years?"

"Various reasons," she shrugged. "College, then I went to work, and Gramps and I seemed to go our separate ways. He's always liked to travel." She smiled whimsically. "Mom always said he had wanderlust, and I guess he has. He's never in one place long enough to call it home." *Which would be the reason I wasn't warned about you,* Megan retorted silently.

"Why didn't you chose an exciting place for vacation rather than here?" Curiosity prompted his question.

She turned the potatoes. "It seemed to be the place to come. I couldn't afford to join Mom and Dad in the Middle East, and I didn't relish the idea of hoofing it through the interior of Mexico with Gramps. So . . ."

"I can't understand why you would choose to spend your vacation alone."

"Don't try," she returned dismissively. "Now it's my turn. What's it like being a dairy farmer?"

While she continued to cook the meal, Alan, responding to her directional comment, steered the conversation into a less personal vein, talking to her about the basic rudiments of dairy farming. In the late dusk of the evening they ate, enjoying their food, lapsing into a period of comfortable silence.

Megan knew that Alan was interested in her only because of his friendship with Joel, and, to be frank, she admitted to herself, she had no more than a friendly interest in him. She certainly didn't want their friendship to develop into anything more than good-neighborliness.

27

She stole a glance at him while he was regarding his food with serious hunger. He wasn't her type. Too tough! Too rugged! Might resort to caveman tactics if he thought it were necessary to get what he wanted. Could be insensitive to a woman's feelings.

Never again would she allow herself to give in to a man, she had resolved eight months ago, and she had been true to her word. After she had been jilted by Shane Herrington she had sworn to protect herself from such hurt again. She had built a facade behind which to hide her shattered heart—a new hairdo, new clothes, and a cool aloofness that seemed to attract men like flies to honey.

Few people knew that the smile never reached her eyes or her heart; few heard the hollowness of her laughter or detected the falseness of her gaiety. She had worked hard to drag herself together piece by piece, working hard to forge a new life for herself, a life that was comfortable and secure.

Her life had been going well until she learned that Shane was being transferred into her office to work for her boss, Farrell Edwards. Now she had to come to grips with herself before she could face Shane again. *That's why, Alan McDonald,* she silently said, *I'm here by myself. I'm seeing if the glue is strong enough to hold me together so that I can meet Shane again.*

Then she heard the thud, and she saw the penny roll across the table. She looked up to encounter at close range —very close range—those mocking green eyes, once again minty and frosty with aloofness. He lifted the penny from the table, holding it between his thumb and index finger.

"Penny for your thoughts."

She stared at him for endless seconds, then at the penny. Finally she confessed, "They're not worth it."

"Usually aren't," he agreed affably, dropping the penny to the table, "but you were so caught up in them I thought for once maybe they were. Want to talk about it?"

She shook her head. "No, I don't want to talk about it." She tried to laugh. "Coming back here has stirred up a lot of childhood memories."

His brows arched questioningly. She had been caught up in more than childhood memories, he knew. Her countenance had been troubled, her eyes heavy with painful remembrances. He ignored what she said. "What are you running from, Megan? Yourself or a man?"

Not surprised at his deduction, she thought for a minute before she answered. "Probably myself. But maybe not from either. I'm really looking for an answer."

He smiled and laid his big, calloused hand over hers. "Don't worry too much over it," he advised. "Problems have a way of clearing themselves up." He scooted the chair back and stood. "While I wash the dishes, why don't you tell me all about it?"

Megan's eyes narrowed, quickly dispelling her past thoughts. "We'll wash dishes together, and I won't tell you anything. I learned a long time ago that men aren't to be trusted."

"Then it's up to me to reeducate you," Alan commented dryly, "and I can understand now why you're out here by yourself." He didn't allow her time to respond to his remarks before he said, "Now, while you wash the dishes, I'll take your friend out for his nightly walk, and you'll be ready to lock up the house when I leave."

Without any more ado, Megan introduced Bismarck to Alan, and the two of them disappeared into the darkness. She finished in the kitchen before they returned, and she walked to the front porch and stood in the cool evening breeze.

Later, when she heard the screen door grate against the porch, she asked, "Why did you decide to make this your home, Alan?"

He laid his hat on the rustic, homemade straight chair

with the cowhide bottom. "I wanted to rear my son out here."

"Your son," she echoed with a start, turning around. "You're married?" Strangely enough she didn't want him to be married; she hadn't figured on his having a wife.

"Was, but not anymore," he tersely stated as he moved to the edge of the porch where she stood. He put both hands into his back hip pockets. Looking at the clear Texas twilight, he commented dryly, "My wife's dead now." He hunched his shoulders slightly. "All that's left of my marriage are Matt, in-laws, and memories."

"Matt," she repeated, "and in-laws?"

"Matthew McDonald, my five-year-old son." He looked down at her and smiled. "And Rosa, Matt's grandmother and my housekeeper. Now will you change your mind about coming to stay with me?"

She shook her head. "Not right now. I'd like to stay here for the time being. I've got to figure a few things out first."

In a light, teasing voice, he asked, "Do you think you could have things figured out by tomorrow evening?"

"Why?" she asked in puzzlement.

"I'd thought about asking you out to dinner."

She pushed a stray lock of hair from her forehead. "Another time perhaps. I thought I'd clean house tomorrow."

"Clean house," he agreed. "You'll still have time for dinner."

She shook her head. "No, I don't think so."

"The house has been cluttered this long," he argued. "Surely another day can't make that much difference." Again she shook her head; then his fingers caught the tip of her chin, stilling her face, tilting it upward. "Just an excuse because you don't trust men and don't want to go out with one."

She didn't reply. She couldn't have lied had she wanted

to, and she wasn't about to admit the truth of his assertion. She stared at him, her mouth parting slightly, her tongue, pink and moist in the pale light that filtered through the opened door, darting out to lick her dry lips.

"No man's worth it, Megan." His words were faint, a mere whisper on the wind, but they were the same words she had heard over and over again during the past eight months.

Tired of these platitudes from people who didn't know how she felt, angry because he would dare be so presumptuous, and highly frustrated because she knew he was right, she wanted to scream. Instead, she jerked her chin from his fingers, which seemed to be burning her skin.

"He may not have been worth it," she agreed coolly, "but it hurts to know that you've been used."

"The best way to forget is to find someone new, Meggie," he advised softly. "Come on," he pleaded in a soft, seductive tone. "You'll have fun. I guarantee that you'll have a good time, and I guarantee that you'll forget all about him."

*I'll bet,* Megan thought, but she just said, "I've already told you, I'm tired, and I'm not fit company for anybody right now. So let's forget about it."

"Let me decide what company I choose to keep," Alan retorted lightly, dismissing her argument. "Maybe I like lousy company."

With a patience she was rapidly losing, Megan searched the cloudy seas of his eyes, searched to confirm her suspicion. What was his purpose? Why was he insisting on her company? Why was he willing to help her forget Shane? Why should he want to soothe her wounded ego?

Just like every other man, she thought bitterly, so sure a few hours of his charm would make her forget months of pain. Well, she decided quickly, she didn't need his help, nor did she want the kind of solace he was offering. With typical male arrogance he was willing to take advantage of her grief to see some kind of strange challenge in her refusal. The impact of this thought incensed her, but it also confirmed her newly gained knowledge of men. They were selfish, egotistical, and arrogant.

"For the last time, Alan," she said, her voice low. "I don't want to go to dinner with you. I would like nothing better than to be left alone." Her gray eyes, rapier-sharp and keen, never left his face. "You see," she pointed out, "contrary to what everyone, including you, believes, I loved Shane Herrington. I loved him very much, and—" He could hear the tears in her voice.

As he surveyed her face, an open book of misery and hurt, he only said, "I doubt that you really loved him, Megan."

"Oh, you do, do you?" she exploded angrily. How dare this man tread continually on the sensitive cords of her heart, question her feelings, make light of her love for Shane. He knew nothing about her or Shane. He didn't know what she did or did not feel.

"But you don't know, do you?" she eventually blurted. "You're like the rest of my so-called friends. Nobody knows but me."

He didn't deem to answer; he just rocked back and forth from heel to toe. *Yes, I know,* he silently contradicted her. *You couldn't have loved a man who was so superficial that he overlooked your budding beauty; you couldn't have loved a man who wasn't capable of knowing you. And only a man who knows you, recognizes you, will ever reach the depths that it takes to find the real Megan Jonas. And you can only love a man who is willing to dig until he finds you.*

*I pity Shane,* Alan thought, *but I'm glad for my sake.* His eyes slowly raked over the pensive woman, proud and regal standing beside him. *I promise you,* Megan Jonas, *I promise myself that I will search until I find you. I will be the man that awakens the real woman inside you.*

Had Megan not been so caught up in her frustration, she would have seen the arrogant promise gleaming in his eyes. As yet she was unaware of him as a man—a man who wanted to possess her, to love her. Yet deep inside she instinctively sensed his challenge, and she found it alluring —he the primitive, she the civilized. But as it was, at that moment, in her conscious thoughts, she refused to acknowledge the powerful, magnetic pull of his personality.

Alan took a deep breath, the penetrating eyes never leaving Megan's profile, and had she again been looking, she would have seen his countenance hardening with calculated determination. Whatever Alan McDonald wanted, he got—one way or the other.

"I still think you ought to accept my invitation, Megan." She heard that subtle command, that covert order.

"I've already told you that I can fend for myself. I'm not going to starve between now and Monday." Her answer was cool and arrogant. During the last eight months she had learned to verbally spar with the best of them.

"Maybe I'm not talking about your hunger for food," he returned softly, the subtle meaning very clear.

Leashing her anger, Megan challenged him. "And I suppose you're the man who can satiate my hunger for love."

He threw back his head and laughed, the deep, rich sound coming from the muscular expanse of his chest. "Oh, Megan, I'm not going to touch that one. I do want you to go with me, and if I answered that, you'd take fright and run away and hide."

Much to Megan's surprise, Alan said no more about going out nor did he plead with her again. It wasn't his nature to beg, and he knew that he would get nowhere with her by doing so. Patience was the key to this game. So when he spoke he assumed indifference.

"Another time."

They stood for a long time, talking and staring at the

star-studded sky before he lifted his Stetson from the back of the chair and flipped it on his head with casual grace. He stepped off the porch and walked toward the pick-up. Lifting his hand in a wave, he said good-bye.

"Be seeing you around."

She lifted her hand and waved, silently mouthing the words which sounded more like a promise than a good-bye.

"Be seeing you around."

# CHAPTER TWO

The days passed swiftly for Megan and much to her surprise Alan didn't ask her out again. Although he came each day to check on her and was friendly, he didn't try to make their relationship more than that. Even when Megan bluntly hinted several times that she would like to meet Matt, Alan nodded his head, never really responding to the suggestion. He seemed to be content with being a good neighbor and in keeping tabs on her for Joel, no more.

And as much as Megan hated to admit it even to herself, she was disappointed. She had reckoned that Alan would be so arrogantly overconfident that he wouldn't wait to test the strength of his charisma on her. She had seen this type before, hadn't she? After all, she thought, Shane was a classic example.

Still, after Shane had dumped her, Megan matured rapidly, and with her new maturity came a different type of beauty, one born of confidence and self-assurance. She held her head a little higher, her chin jutting forward, her lips curved into an illusive smile. It made people wonder. Was it a smile? Did it come from the heart? Did it really touch those full, sensuous lips? Her carriage was more graceful, and she possessed a lithe economy of movement. Her gray eyes sparkled with a vital life force; they were enigmatic, containing a hint of intimate promise, an arrogant blaze of defiance, and they were cloaked with an icy veil of indifference.

It would be nice to spend the evening away from the house, she daydreamed, walking into the kitchen to get herself a glass of tea, and while she was letting her fancy fly, she imagined herself with Alan as her escort. Even in his jeans, boots, and western shirts he was strikingly handsome. Not debonair and elegant like Shane, but outdoorsy, rugged, purely physical. She sighed; he was deliciously physical.

Her eyes gleamed with satisfaction when she imagined how women would watch him as they walked through a restaurant, a nightclub, or down the street. And he would be the ideal escort. She imagined his seductive smile, the male attentiveness, his pleasure in pleasing, the exciting titillation of her senses, his expert guidance into the splendid mysteries of intimacy.

She unconsciously lifted her glass to her lips and sipped her tea, her thoughts running wild. What kind of woman would Alan want? He had told her Saturday evening that he didn't mind lousy company, but she knew better than that. He would want a woman who was on her toes, and, she added to herself, not one just standing in high heels. It would be a battle of wills from the beginning, slowly merging into a sensual battle of the minds, deliciously melding into that primeval battle between man and woman, that neverending struggle for domination and sweet surrender.

She shivered, goosebumps running up and down her spine as she lost herself in fantasy. Alan would be exciting, and he would excite—his glances, that one-sided smile, the covert touches. And she would play the part of the coquette—her leg casually grazing his, only to be moved quickly, her fingers lightly and accidentally touching him. She would return the smile, slowly lower the thick dark lashes, hiding the promise, exultant in the dare.

The crunching sound of a car on the driveway jostled her back to the cold reality of her world, and she walked to the opened door in the living room, flipping up the latch on the screen. She could hardly believe her eyes. The leading man of her reverie was here in person, whistling happily, strolling across the lawn as if he hadn't a care in the world.

The smile that welled from deep within Megan still played across her face, and her eyes were smoky soft and warm, bemusing yet lingering. Pushing open the screen, she greeted him.

"Hello, Farmer McDonald," she teased lightly, her voice a husky contralto. "I'm glad to see you."

The whistling stopped, and Alan returned the smile, noting the stardust in her eyes, the smile that blatantly bedazzled, the welcome in the greeting. His eyes, though wary, were bright with anticipation. Evidently his timing was right.

"I'm glad I stopped by too," he quipped in return. He looked thirstily at her glass of tea. "Got any more of that brewed?"

"Sure do," she returned with a laugh and a toss of her beautiful hair. "Want a glass?"

Alan peeled off his gloves, throwing them onto the sofa along with his hat. "I feel like I could drink a gallon of it." He followed her into the kitchen. "I've been putting up a new fence, and I'm just about tuckered out. Just about the time I thought I was finished for the day, Fowler called and wants me to come help him unload some new equipment, so here I go."

By this time Megan had filled his glass with tea and was handing it to him. Taking the glass, he turned it up, drinking long and appreciatively of the ice-cold amber beverage. Unable to resist, her gaze moved along the column of his strong, tan throat, down to the patch of dark hair just visible at the opening of his shirt.

"This hits the spot, Megan." He pulled the chair from under the table and sat down, leaning back wearily. "Since I've got to go through town, I wondered if there was anything I could get for you—groceries, supplies, that sort of thing."

Megan, standing in front of the sink, sipped her tea slowly, shaking her head. "No, I bought all I needed Monday when I went in."

He nodded, lifting the pitcher to refill his glass, again quaffing deeply to quench his thirst. Megan watched as he drank, wishing he would ask her to accompany him. She was bored, and she would enjoy getting away for a little while. The idea that she would like to spend the time with Alan McDonald was quickly brushed aside as one would brush aside an annoying fly, hoping it wouldn't return to torment.

After another glass of tea and more idle conversation Alan stood, grating the chair as his legs pushed it back.

"Guess I'd better get going. Joe's gonna wonder what happened." Slowly he sauntered into the living room, leading the way, looking at the room with studied care. "I don't know that I've ever seen this house so clean and homey. You've done a good job, Meggie."

"Thanks," she grinned, still hoping, still wishing that he would ask her to go with him.

He leaned over the couch, picked up the gloves, stuffed them into his hip pocket, and flipped his hat on his head, tugging it in front a time or two to adjust it.

"When's vacation over?" he asked absently, giving Megan the impression that he wasn't that interested.

Probably he wondered when his goodwill visits could

38

end, she thought. "I'll be leaving Friday morning. I've got to report to work on Monday."

"Not long," he whistled soundlessly. "Your days as a woman of leisure are just about over." He took a few more steps, stopping in the doorway, leaning indolently against the frame. "If I'm not sounding too . . . fatherly, and if I'm not prying into your personal life, I'd like to ask you a question."

Megan's finely arched brows rose queryingly. "Go ahead." She couldn't imagine what he wanted to know, but she was hoping.

"Have you solved all the great problems of your life?"

When she heard the question disappointment washed over her. She had hoped for more, dared to hope for more. Unbeknownst to her, she sighed her regret, the clarion sound carrying to Alan's ears.

He folded his arms across his chest, that mischievous grin racing through his eyes, taking residence in his lips. Maybe Megan Jonas had wallowed in self-pity long enough. Perhaps she's ready for people. *This is the time for me to act,* he thought. He had been aware of the hope generating in her eyes, and he had felt her silent imploring. But he had to be sure. He didn't have the time for a mistake; he must handle her with tender caution.

"See you later," he said, pushing on the screen and stepping into the warm spring afternoon.

His footsteps echoed across the room as he stepped onto the porch, and he willed Megan to initiate the next move. All she did, however, was to follow him to the door and stand there watching as he slowly crossed the lawn.

She stared at the checkered blue shirt, damp with perspiration, across the broad muscle-corded back, the bulging biceps that looked as if they had the power to hold up the world if Atlas ever needed help. She couldn't let Alan leave, but she had too much pride to ask him to take her with him. After all, she recalled dryly, he had ignored her suggestions about meeting Matt.

Then the answer came. A bolt of lightning couldn't have galvanized her into action any quicker. Just as his hand closed over the door handle of the truck, she raced over the porch, down the steps, and across the lawn, calling to him.

"Alan! Alan, wait a minute." She stood, looking at him, screwing her face against the glare of the sun. "I'd like for you to come for dinner tonight. I'd like to repay you for your hospitality that first night, and—"

She dropped her eyes, the thick brown lashes batting coquettishly. Then at the right moment she swept them upward, revealing two wide, soft, beguiling gray eyes, full of invitation and that hint of promise. And even though Alan was no novice when it came to the battle of the sexes, he was enchanted by her antics. He wasn't at all adverse to playing the game.

"I'd like to make amends for my rudeness," she continued on a softer, evocative note. *Resist that if you can,* she thought, riding high on the wind of her exhilarated recklessness.

He leaned against his hand, which was still curled around the metal of the door handle, and he stared at the woman standing in front of him. His green eyes blatantly raked over her figure, causing faint color to fuse into her cheeks. *She's ready,* he figured. *She's tired of being left alone; she bored; and she's ready for my company.* At the same time, he figured, *anybody's* company would do.

It galled him to know this, to know that at this moment anyone would have suited Megan's purpose. She was lonely and as a result was playing a dangerous game that she was certain to lose. Yet this was better than nothing. He shook his head, swallowing the bitter taste of truth.

"Sorry, Megan, I'd love to, but I'm driving into Del Rio for dinner tonight. Some other time perhaps."

With finality in his words and gesture, he turned, opened the door, and heaved himself as if weightless into the cab of the truck, banging the door after himself. He leaned over, switched on the ignition, and revved the engine. Then, and only then, did his head turn in Megan's direction.

Struggling valiantly to keep her disappointment from showing, she smiled and shrugged as if it were of no consequence. "Another time," she agreed indifferently, her heart knowing there would be no other time. "It doesn't really matter." She turned and walked toward the porch, calling softly to Bismarck, who was running around the yard.

But it did matter, she thought, and she was more disappointed than she wanted to admit even to herself. She was hurt; the pain was sharp and cutting, a slicing pain in her midsection, her heart tight, as if two walls were shoving in on each side of it. Her breathing was shallow; a veil of tears shielded her eyes.

She put her foot on the bottom step when she suddenly heard her name called out. She stopped, indicating that she'd heard it, but she didn't turn in the direction from which it came. She didn't want him to see her face—an open book for him to read.

"Would you like to ride over to Fowler's with me?"

The faint words rode on the wind, and she wasn't sure if she heard them or not. Perhaps it was her fancifulness running rampant. Holding herself in check, she managed to slowly turn, blinking back her tears, staring at him for a minute before she answered, swallowing the lump in her throat.

He searched through the distance, trying to see her face, looking for a clue to her feelings, but she had masked them, lowered the shutter to the mirror of her soul, and he couldn't find an inkling to betray her emotions. For a

41

minute he wondered, almost held his breath. Would she go? Or had he imagined that she wanted to go?

She bounced onto the second step, still facing him. Her lips gently curved upward, parting, the edge of her even white teeth showing, her smile as bright as the early morning sunshine in the spring. Her smile was the sun of his day; her happiness the rays, radiating from her eyes, her very soul, inspiring her movement, guiding her. She danced up the steps, laughingly calling back to him.

"Let me get my purse and lock up the house. I'd love to go with you."

She scampered through the house, yanking her shirt off, hastily pulling another on, kicking out of her shorts, tugging on a pair of jeans, brushing her hair, slipping her feet into a pair of better sandals, doing a million things at once and fumbling through all of them. She was afraid that he'd change his mind, tire of waiting for her, and leave. Finally, however, she was locking the door, racing toward the truck, climbing in, grinning at him. Happily she squirmed into position as he drove away.

"Where do the Fowlers live?" she asked curiously as Alan swerved out of the drive onto the narrow dirt road.

He chuckled. "I'll tell you, but I don't know how much it'll mean." Succinctly he gave her detailed directions to Joe Fowler's farm.

She joined in with his laughter. "You're right. I still don't know."

She listened as Alan began to quietly talk about the small rural community of Los Nogalitos, the people and the land. He talked about the likes and the dislikes of the residents; he regaled her with their unassumed and unpretentious interests and their accomplishments. And as Megan listened she learned that Alan had a deep-seated love for this place and its people.

In so many ways he reminded her of Gramps. With surprise she cocked her head and looked at Alan, never having thought of him in this light before. It wasn't a physical resemblance, she decided, chewing on her thumbnail absently as she closely scrutinized him. It was a character similarity; their makeup was very much alike. Both of them were self-willed, arrogant, and self-confident to the point of being conceited. And each was accustomed to having his own way—dictating, demanding, manipulating, cajoling, whatever means it took. A benevolent tyrant!

Her eyes were cloudy with her bemused speculation, and her lips were parted, her teeth lightly biting on her tongue, when Alan glanced in her direction.

"And what are you thinking?" he asked, not taking his eyes off the road for long.

She replied truthfully. "I was thinking about how much you remind me of Gramps."

Alan chuckled good-naturedly, but Megan could hear the bitter undercurrent. "I don't think I like being compared to old men all the time, Megan. It seems to label me as a meddlesome old man rather than an aspiring lover." He heard Megan's rich gurgle of laughter, and he looked over, smiling at her. "It might be more flattering if you compared me to your father rather than your grandfather. At least he's younger."

Megan laughed again. "You don't remind me of Dad at all." Then she sobered. "I guess through the years I've been closer to Gramps than I have with Dad." She explained, "Dad's always worked abroad more than he's been home, and Mom's always gone with him. So Gramps has played an important role in my life."

"Why didn't you travel with your parents?" Alan asked with genuine interest.

"I did for a while," Megan returned wistfully, "but then I began to feel like that proverbial fifth wheel. I didn't like the social whirl that Mom and Dad seemed to live in and for. I wanted to come home. And through the years home came to mean Gramps and wherever we happened to be roaming."

"Year around?" he asked.

Megan laughed. "Of course not. During the school year we lived in Dallas and saved our roaming until the summer. Each year we'd come out here to Los Nogalitos." Her voice trailed into silence as she lost herself in the happy memories of her childhood with Joel. "And then it ended," she supplied succinctly.

"Not really ended," Alan amended. "You just grew up and home meant more than Joel and roaming. Joel recognized that, and so should you."

Megan nodded. "I guess that's right," she agreed quietly. "After I graduated and went to work for Zelco, Gramps helped me find an apartment. He was determined that I would stand on my own two feet. He wanted me to be as independent as he was." Again Alan heard the deep gurgle of laughter. "That's what I mean, Alan, you remind me so much of Gramps."

"And I said that's not too flattering," Alan asserted with humor.

Although Megan accepted his words good-naturedly, she heard that twinge of seriousness in them. She smiled fully, rejoicing in her prowess as a woman able to arouse a man—this man. He wasn't as unaffected by her opinion as he would have her believe. This knowledge filled her with a surge of intuitive feminine seduction. If she wanted to, she could have Alan eating out of the palm of her hand. Reveling in the grip of her discovery of herself as a seductress, she decided that she wanted to tame this man, feel him quiver under her touch, obey her command.

Again Alan glanced at her just in time to see the smile that curved her lips, to see the purposeful gleam in her eyes. It was as if she had slapped his cheek with a glove, throwing it at his feet, defying him to pick it up. So physical was her message that he answered it aloud.

"I'm willing to play your game, Megan, but consider well before we begin. I mean to win. If I should happen to lose, I'll ask for no mercy, but if I win, I'll give no mercy. Understood?"

The words were velvety soft, soothing to Megan's high-keyed emotions, yet they offered her the exhilaration and excitement of the duel. She had challenged him; he had picked up the glove. Now it was her turn; he was waiting.

Megan's voice was seductively soft when she spoke. "There's always a first time to lose, you know."

"Remember those words," he enjoined with a chuckle, speaking in the same tones as she. "You may have to eat them one of these days."

Megan's laugh, cool and trilling, filled the truck with soft music. "Aren't you afraid that perhaps, Mr. McDonald, you may have to eat humble pie yourself?"

The gentle but serious banter continued until they reached the small farm, and while Alan and Joe Fowler loaded the equipment, Megan sat on the front porch of the house and visited with Joe's wife, Peggy. For one of the few times in Megan's life, time seemed to fly, and she was totally unprepared for Alan's appearance.

"It's about time for us to go," he announced as he turned the corner of the house. "I've still got plenty to do before I hit the road for Del Rio."

Following him, Joe agreed with a hearty laugh. "Yep, Megan, he can go now. I've got about all the work outa him that I can."

Peggy stood, inviting them to dinner. "Don't reckon you'd want to stay for supper, would you? There's plenty, and we'd be mighty happy to have you."

Joe agreed with Peggy and joined her persuasion, but Alan continued to shake his head. "Love to, Joe, but another time. I promised Rosa that I'd pick up Elena, and I want to clean up." He winked at Joe. "Got a heavy date tonight."

Joe grinned. "I understand. Another time then."

In the rush of the good-byes, Megan didn't have time to question Alan about Elena, and she didn't have time to dwell on it either, but wonder and curiosity did fleet temporarily through her mind. Then her thoughts were hastily brushed aside so she could listen to the soft droning of Peggy as she walked to the truck.

But once Megan was seated in the truck, farewells said, the truck moving, she began to cogitate. Who was Elena? Why did Alan have to pick her up? Why hadn't he said something about her earlier?

"Why so quiet, Megan?" Alan asked, closing the distance between Fowler's place and town.

"Just wondering about Elena," she replied, her words becoming an extension of her thoughts.

"Rosa's daughter," he commented. "She's just coming in from college, and today is her first day to work at the pharmacy." He went on to explain. "She's worked there throughout her high school days, and she's going to work there through the summer."

"You've never mentioned her before," Megan remarked, wondering why. Wondering why she was so hurt about it, and wondering why he'd never mentioned her. Perhaps Elena was the person whom he'd been telling Joe about. Maybe that was his "hot date" for the night. Perhaps Elena was his type of woman.

"No." The word could have been a question or a quip. Megan wasn't sure. Then he said, "Neither of us has shared too much personal information with the other, have we?"

Megan grinned, although her cheeks were tinged with a small amount of pink, and she nodded. During the past four days she and Alan had indulged in social niceties, casual questions, and equally casual answers, trite and senseless for the most part.

By this time he had parked in front of the pharmacy and

was honking the horn, and one of the most beautiful women Megan had ever seen was walking out of the double glass doors. Her black hair, cut in a shag, gently framed her face, and her mouth was full and red, curving into a petulant smile. Yet her lips were sensuous, lips any man would crave to taste. She looked as if she had just stepped out of a fashion magazine. Her gauzy beige dress was carefully draped over her voluptuous figure, clinging in all the right places, complemented by her gold earrings and belt and her dark brown macramé high-heeled shoes.

As long as Elena stared at Alan, the eyes retained their smile, but when she saw Megan sitting in the passenger seat, her smile vanished and venom belched from her smoky eyes. She opened the door, speaking churlishly to Alan, looking beyond Megan as if she weren't sitting there.

"Mother said you were coming to pick me up, but she said nothing about your bringing someone with you." The words were vehement with accusation.

Alan lifted his brows and frowned, not liking Elena's rudeness, but rather than make an issue of it at the present, he said, "Elena, I'd like for you to meet Joel's granddaughter, Megan Jonas."

Elena opened the door and sat down, in no hurry to acknowledge Alan's introduction. Eventually, however, she did manage to spit a curt greeting. Then she turned her full attention to Alan, her words warm and petulantly chiding. "Why didn't you say anything about bringing Megan with you?"

"Because it was none of your business," Alan softly retorted, an abrupt curtness residing in his answer. He intended to have a reckoning with this young lady as soon as they arrived home.

Megan, sitting between the two, was grinning. Both of them were furious, albeit for two different reasons. Elena was angry because Alan had brought her along and had destroyed the intimate journey home that Elena had planned, and Alan was angry that Elena would dare question his rights.

Megan decided to speak, thinking she might be able to avert the brewing storm. "I'm glad to meet you, Elena. Alan's been telling me something about you."

Elena turned those coal black eyes toward Megan, letting them rove disdainfully over her old jeans and cotton shirt. "Did he?" The question was unnecessary and filled with sarcasm. Megan knew that Elena couldn't have cared less. Now Elena smiled. "I wish I could say the same, but he hasn't said a word about you."

"Elena," Alan warned.

Elena laughed. "Just joking, Alan." Again her eyes raked over Megan. "Actually he did tell Mother and me that he was worried about your staying at Joel's by yourself." She chuckled. "See you made it all right."

Megan returned Elena's scornful glare with a candid gaze that caused Elena to lower her eyes. She couldn't meet those cold blades of steel, which were burnished and sharp, the edge ready for cutting and trimming.

"Yes, Elena." Her words were sugary sweet, and she purred with the innocence of a tiny kitten. "I made it all right. As you can see, I'm old enough to take care of myself." *And I'm old enough to be more cautious,* she added silently. Casting a side glance at the tight profile of the driver, she added another postscript. *And I'm intelligent enough to avoid getting Farmer McDonald this angry with me when I've noplace to run.*

Elena's eyes flashed, and she snapped, "I figured you'd be okay." The poutish smile pulled her lips derisively. "I told Alan that it was useless to worry about you, but he had to tell Mother and both of them worried." She looked down the end of her nose at Megan. "Both of them want you to stay with us." Disdain coated her next words. "Alan should have known by looking that you were past

48

the age of needing a chaperone." She sneered. "Alan acted as if you were a baby who needed protecting."

Alan's face contorted in anger, and Megan could see the constraining whiteness around the corners of his mouth that testified to his barely restrained emotions. Before Alan could retort, however, Megan chuckled. She had handled worse than Elena, and she could see through the childish outburst. Elena was jealous—so jealous she could hardly see straight, so jealous she refused to rationalize very well. *Well,* Megan decided with a low chuckle, *I'll just give you some food for thought. I'll show you how it feels to wear the same shoe.*

"No," Megan conceded with good grace, "I'm not THAT young. I'm twenty-five." She glanced at Elena. Two could play this game. She squinted her eyes and studied Elena's face closely. "I'd say you're not too many years older than I am."

"Of all the nerve," Elena spit, her cheeks red with anger. "I have you know I'm only twenty years old."

"I'm sorry," Megan wailed dramatically, rolling her eyes, "I surely didn't know. You do look much older, you know. Perhaps it's the way you dress, the way you talk."

Alan chuckled. Elena sulked in her corner of the truck, peering out the side window, and Megan smiled with satisfaction. When Alan's laughter died down, he glanced over at the woman seated next to him, silently congratulating her, a new feeling invading his large frame—an exhilaration and an appreciation for the wit and wisdom of the little hellcat who was sitting beside him, very nonchalantly purring over her victory.

*She won't be easily conquered,* Alan repeated to himself, *but that would make the mating more gratifying.* His mastery of her would be sweet indeed. Sweet for the both of them; sweet for the final culmination. The purring first, the snarling, the growling, the clawing and scratching, finally that guttural cry of the feline species when she's chosen her mate—the sheathing of the claws.

"I think, Elena, you got what you deserved," Alan asserted eventually. "I knew that one of these days your barbed tongue would get you into trouble."

Elena didn't bother to answer. She continued to stare out the window, swearing vehemently to herself that she would get even one of these days. Megan wouldn't go unpunished for having treated her like this, reducing her to an object of ridicule. Why did Megan have to come? Just when Alan was beginning to see her as a woman.

The atmosphere in the truck was tense, and the trip home was not nearly as pleasant as the earlier one had been, but Megan still enjoyed her occasional sparring with Alan, and both seemed to forget that Elena was balled tightly in her corner. When he stopped in front of Joel's place, he let Megan out on his side and walked her to the door.

"I'm glad you came," he said, backing down the steps, "and I'm certainly sorry I can't take you up on that dinner tonight, but I've already made plans."

Megan smiled ruefully, her disappointment from earlier in the day once again enshrouding her, becoming her garment for the evening. "It's okay," she murmured, although she knew it wasn't. She turned, slipping the key into the lock. When she heard the click, she moved her head, casting Alan a partial glance over her shoulder. "If you've made plans, you've made plans." Dropping the key into her purse, her mouth curved upward, but she wasn't smiling; she was merely going through the motions. "Have fun," she said.

"Usually do," he quipped lightly.

Megan stood framed in the open door, watching him as he slowly sauntered back to the truck, his flippant words slapping her in the face. Of course he would have a good time. Why shouldn't he? He climbed in, said something to

50

Elena which caused her to laugh and caused Megan's stomach to knot with unhappiness—unhappiness or jealousy, she wondered. Maybe both!

Then he revved the engine, slowly moving away. He turned his head one last time, looked at Megan, and as an afterthought lifted his hand and waved. Dully Megan returned the gesture half-heartedly, spinning around saucily, walking into the house to spend another evening alone. But she stopped. Did she hear the truck backing up? Did she hear Alan calling to her? Quickly she turned. Yes, he was backing up, and yes, he was calling to her.

"Do you want to go with me?"

*Do I want to go with you?* she cried to herself. *Better yet, would I not want to go with you?* She stood as if in animated suspension for a second or two, enjoying her exultant stupefaction. This is what she had been wanting. But she was afraid.

She liked Alan, liked him too much. Could she hold out for the duration of an evening in the intimacy of the truck, the restaurant, the good nights? While she waited and thought, he got out of the truck, leaving the motor running and Elena fuming, to return to the porch.

"Do you?"

His eyes swept over each feature of her face, and it was as if he were touching her—the wisps of hair that escaped her combs, her gray eyes, her mouth, her chin. Then his gaze dropped to the gentle contours of her breasts, the satiny swell that was slightly exposed by the scooped neckline of her shirt.

Again he spoke, his words a sedative to her languid decision, a narcotic to her already drugged senses. "You'll enjoy being with me if you'll give yourself half a chance."

She had to hand it to him; he was persistent, turning every event into his advantage, always pinning her to the wall with those eyes, always standing himself in the best vantage point. Her own eyes shifted to his, and she ran through the green grassland, frolicking in the gentle summer breeze, losing and not wanting to find herself. She opened her mouth to speak, but no words came.

Alan's voice, husky and gravelly, wafted over her numbed senses. "All men aren't like him, Megan."

"They aren't," she whispered, still wandering in the verdant meadow, her eyes never leaving the beauty of his.

"You can't punish all men or yourself because of one."

"I can't," she whispered again, trancelike, trusting him, wanting him to join her in the lucent greenness.

He shook his head, the gentle movement back and forth breaking the hypnotic hold. "I'm different, Megan, and I'll treat you differently."

*Conceit,* she thought hazily, not minding in the least.

"You'll enjoy our evening, and you'll enjoy being with me."

*Arrogant,* she silently charged, still not minding.

"I promise."

*You promise,* she repeated on hushed breath.

He saw her indecision; he saw the dreamy wonder in her eyes, the hazy fascination on her face. His hand, of its own volition, rose; his fingers, feather light, splayed her cheeks, the tip of each finger exciting a hundred exposed nerve endings, sending sharp, erotic messages throughout her system.

He smiled; without trying he had won. Megan was ready to fall into his arms. She was his for the taking; he could do what he wished with her. How sweet the taste of victory, he thought with typical male egotism.

He should have hooded his eyes, Megan thought with a start, reading the arrogant conceit and gloating she saw there. But she was glad that he hadn't. She had been warned, salvaged, perhaps saved. She wouldn't let him play with her like this. She wasn't a toy to be played with, cast aside when tired of, thrown into a toy box never to be seen again.

He saw her eyes narrow, and he could see the steely glint; he could feel her icy retreat. *God,* he thought, *does she truly hate men? Is she adverse to them altogether?* Then he saw that tiny flicker, saw it deep in the depth of those gray eyes. He realized that this flicker of emotion was so small that even she was unaware of it. Like a bolt of lightning it struck him. She's afraid!

The discovery was as shattering as it was startling; conversely, it was exhilarating. Megan was afraid! Why? Because she'd never tasted the fruit of love, delved into the garden of sexual pleasure, drank of the nectar of sensual touch, ate of the goodness of desire until she was replete.

*She's afraid of being attracted to another man, of falling in love. She's afraid to climb that mountain to discover what love is all about, afraid to scan the new horizon of love with a man who can meet her needs, match her wants—fulfill them,* he thought.

Alan was glad that Megan hadn't explored this garden of want and desire with anyone else; he was glad that he would be her guide. He wouldn't have liked the idea of her falling out of Shane's arms immediately into another man's, even if he were that man. He was glad that she had saved herself for him. Although she had done it through no knowledge of her own, he was still glad. He would appreciate her; he would enjoy her, give pleasure and receive the same from her in equal measure.

"Scared?" he jeered softly, smiling when she winced visibly.

Megan didn't answer. She continued to stare into his face. She had cause to be afraid, she thought. Alan McDonald was planning methodically and calculatedly to seduce her senses, her emotions, her heart, and her body. She had seen it in his eyes. He wanted her, and he wouldn't stop until he possessed her—body and soul.

Again he mocked her. This seemed to be the only way

to jar her out of that cocoon into which she had retreated eight months ago.

"Scaredy-cat!"

The truck horn blared out, but Megan was completely oblivious to the noise and to the other woman. She shook her head, refusing to lose Alan to the present and refusing to let him know that she was afraid.

"No, I'm not afraid to go with you. I'm just tired of people telling me what I do or don't need—psychoanalyzing me. So far I haven't seen one doctor's shingle hanging out. Yet each one of them, including you, is willing to diagnose my case and to prescribe the cure."

He emitted that quiet chuckle that she was beginning to love. "No, Megan," he denied, "that's not all there is to it. You're afraid. Mostly you're afraid. You're afraid that you'll like me, afraid that you'll more than like me."

"Alan, for God's sake, come on. I'm burning up," Elena bellowed from the truck. Alan raised his hand, acknowledging her, but he didn't take his eyes or his attention from Megan.

As far as Megan was concerned, Elena didn't exist. Only she and Alan did. Her face was lit up with a dazzling smile, and devilment lurked in the hidden depths of those gray eyes that had so recently been remote and unreadable.

"Elena's burning up," Megan taunted, her light tone carrying her double meaning.

"Probably," he returned absently. "It'll do her good." His green eyes had darkened, and Megan shivered when she saw the turbulent gleam in them. "Changing the subject because you're afraid."

"I doubt it, Farmer McDonald," she purred softly, Elena forgotten once again. "I've built up a strong resistance, and, may I add, a strong distaste for men like you."

She wouldn't admit—at least not willingly—that she was attracted to him. She hadn't been afraid of Shane.

There had been no reason, she suddenly realized. He hadn't affected her like Alan did. But she was afraid of Alan. His eyes could penetrate her very soul; his body could dictate her every response; he seemed to know and understand her like no other person did.

She feared this primitive, rugged man. This man who appeared to be so simple, yet had a depth that she hadn't yet reached, hadn't yet discovered—could only discover if she became his mate. Or was the correct word *playmate?*

She feared that in one move he would strip away her defenses piece by piece. No mercy given. That's what the man had said. He would demand a total, a complete response to that raw, untamed streak in him. Would he then leave her naked and alone?

"Want to bet?" His taunt was soft, but the steely challenge was there.

Megan's smile widened, and she nodded, excitement welling up inside her, daring her to cross the line of caution, leaving it far behind.

"I'll bet."

She threw her head back, her eyes gleaming metallic-hard, rapier-sharp. The silvery circlets reminded him of a sword drawn, its blade glistening in the sunlight, the ominous sharpness ready to draw blood, to vanquish the intruder. She was prepared to do battle, to fight to the end, to relinquish nothing willingly.

His eyes answered her messages. They glinted with the same defiance; they sparkled with the same purpose. Megan read it easily, answering in kind. She would go with him, but he wouldn't make her care. He wouldn't tear down that barrier of indifference she had so painstakingly constructed.

Somewhere in the outer periphery of their world, Megan heard a truck door open. Then she heard Alan's angry snarl.

"Elena, you stay right where you are. I'll be there when

I'm ready, and I mean it." His eyes, cold and hard, flew to the young girl who was climbing out of the truck. "Stay right where you are. I'll be there in a minute." The grating authority quelled Elena's spirit, and she meekly slipped back into the truck, closing the door.

The green eyes now lit on Megan, who was proudly flaunting herself, preening herself because Alan preferred to be with her. And he felt the blood surge through his veins, basking in the glorious exultance of the victor as he moves into the conquered territory. *Now to take the captive maiden, the conquered queen,* he thought. He would assault her emotions; he would make her desire him.

It had been a long time—a long time, indeed, since he'd felt a challenge like this, since he'd been more than casually attracted to a woman. For the past four or five years he'd been content with fleeting affairs—allowing intimacy to a degree, making or accepting no commitment beyond the mutual pleasure shared at that particular moment.

With a newly gained boldness, Megan smiled candidly into Alan's face, recognizing the conqueror's glint in the set of his face, knowing that she was part of the booty. But her eyes were openly defiant. Her message to him was clarion-clear.

*If you get me,* she said, *you'll have to take me. I'll never give in willingly.* Shane hadn't tamed her, she realized with a giddy feeling of triumph. He hadn't come near to taming her, she thought in astonishment, not having time to dwell on her discovery, as she was too intent on her duel with the farmer.

She smiled again, boldly flirting with the pursuer, tingling with delightful apprehension, wondering what it would be like to be captured, ravished . . . and, to her shocked amazement, to be loved by Alan McDonald. The pink tip of her tongue ran along the full roundness of her lower lip, the sensuous planes of the upper one, glazir them with a thick sheen of moisture, garbing them in an alluring sensuality.

"Formal or informal?" There was no doubt and no hesitation. The words rang clearly and truly.

"Informal." The same decisiveness. "Will an hour give you time enough to get dressed?"

"Plenty."

He walked to the edge of the porch, his hand automatically going to the brim of his Stetson, fiddling with it, cocking it just right on his forehead. One foot was on the highest step, the second resting on the lowest one. He looked back at her.

"I like promptness in a woman."

She pulled on the screen door, leaning her back against its narrow width, holding it open with her weight. She surveyed him with an arrogant sweep of her eyes, her voice seductively sweet when she answered.

"What you want and what you get, Farmer McDonald, are two different things."

His smile didn't change, but Megan could see the laughter shining in his eyes, and she knew he was well pleased with her retort. She knew as well as he that both of them were looking forward to the evening ahead of them. Both anticipated a victory. Both wondered who would win.

"I always get what I want, Megan Jonas. Always." He paused. "Remember that."

Then he was gone, and Megan was watching the truck disappear into the beautiful south Texas horizon. Only at that moment did she spare a jot of pity for the beautiful, petulant girl who had been sulking in the truck. She could only guess what would happen when the two of them were securely trapped in the privacy of the cab. She grinned. Alan deserved it. But reason quickly asserted itself. Alan is capable of giving as well as taking, she remembered.

Her heart added the hasty whisper, not only in dealing with a misbehaved child, but in giving to the woman he

57

loves, giving of himself. This revelation warmed Megan with its intensive penetration, causing her to indulge in rampant daydreaming, wild, sensual, evocative.

The hour couldn't pass soon enough!

## CHAPTER THREE

In a dreamy, meditative languorousness, Megan ambled through the living room into the bedroom, yanking her shirt over her head, unzipping and kicking out of her jeans. Carrying the discarded items in her hands, she walked into the bathroom where she shed her underwear, dropping all the clothing carelessly into the clothes hamper. She leaned over the old-fashioned four-legged tub and turned on the taps, liberally adding bath oil.

Sinking into the hot water, she toasted her body while her mind continued its mental reverie. For the first time in a good while—*let's see*, she thought, *eight months*—she was looking forward to her evening out, and she would treat herself and Alan to first class. She wouldn't wear pants, although she had brought some of her designer jeans. She would wear her tiered skirt and the matching floral blouse, which was bright and splashy.

When she was red as a lobster, and her skin was hot to the touch, she stepped out of the tub, leisurely drying herself, enjoying the gentle massage of the towel. Dressing for Alan would be fun, she thought with devilish delight.

She could envision his face when he saw her in something besides her old faded jeans and T-shirts.

She pulled the nylon panties up her sleek, copper-toned legs and over her hips and buttocks. She cupped her breasts with a lacy front-snap bra. Then she stepped into the bright red skirt and hurriedly buttoned up her blouse. As she brushed her mane of luxuriant dark brown hair, she slipped into a pair of multicolored sandals, which complemented her outfit. Had it been cooler, she would have let her hair wave gently around her face, but since it was rather warm, she pulled it back on each side, securing it with two matching combs. Pleased with the results, she was pirouetting in front of the mirror when she heard the truck crunch across the gravel driveway.

Grabbing her purse, she ran through the house, turning off the lights and telling Bismarck good night, assuring him that she'd be back soon. She had just switched off the living room light and was locking the door when Alan lithely sprang onto the porch. She turned, dropping the key into her purse at the same time that his calloused hand grasped her elbow—a proprietary touch that left Megan in no doubt to Alan's opinion and intentions.

Her arm tingled from the burning brand of his electrified touch. Her blood coursed through her veins, through every cell in her body. Her pulses hammered; her heart palpitated erratically. She felt as if she were struggling to breathe. Never had she felt like this before, not even when Shane had touched her. Refusing to give Alan the satisfaction of knowing how much he affected her, though, she gave the appearance of being composed and in control.

Still she cast a side glance to see if he was affected by her nearness as much as she was by his. Drats, she cursed him. If he were, he certainly was giving no indication. Then he looked down at her and smiled—that smile which

60

made her feel as if it were hers alone, a smile that he had given to no other.

He opened the door on his side of the truck and helped her in. Scurrying to the opposite corner, she smiled to herself. When she peered at him from under half-closed lids, she smirked openly. He'd have to fight for any territory he gained tonight. And he had another thought coming if he figured she was going to nestle herself against his powerful frame, willingly allowing him to seduce her with his nearness.

He tried to look reprimandingly at her, but his lips began to twitch and in spite of himself he chuckled. "Scaredy-cat," he jeered, levering himself inside the cab. He crooked a finger at her, but Megan shook her head.

She chuckled softly with him, her lips curving naturally and her eyes sparkling with excitement and anticipation. "No," she replied emphatically, "I'm not afraid and, no, I'm not going to sit close to you." His eyes mocked her. "Just cautious," she went on, adding on the same soft note, "And you'd better try a new technique. That one's worn thin. At least give me a mark for being a quick learner."

"I foresee a pleasurable evening ahead, Meggie," Alan affirmed. "There's nothing I enjoy more than a good workout with a woman."

"May I remind you," she corrected on a breathy note, "this is not just a sparring match. It's win or lose, my lord."

"Winner take all," Alan added, his eyes catching hers.

Small tongues of desire lapped in his emerald eyes, and Megan saw the latent heat, the potential fire that he promised. The eyes, warm and green, seductive green ocean billows washing in on her, drowning reason, assiduously roved over her face, his lips moving or giving the illusion of moving, sensuously, erotically awakening her senses, driving her to a frenzied pitch, touching but not touching, titillating, tantalizing, tormenting. He devoured her, singeing her with only the embers of his desire. Dear God, she thought almost fearfully, what could he do to her if he were blazing with that same desire.

"Agreed, Megan?" he taunted. "Winner take all." The words hung in the tense, crackling air.

She opened her mouth, her tongue slowly peeping out, slipping over the red fullness, leaving a film of seductive moisture with which to capture her prey. It wouldn't take much, she thought, for those tiny leaping flames to be fanned into a blazing inferno. She looked at the green eyes—imagining, as it were, the forest fire—a fire burning out of control, devouring all that was in its way, a fire by which she could be charred, burned, consumed, even destroyed, but what divine pleasure through it all.

The thought horrified her, and this fear was reflected in her eyes, but before Alan could read this, she dropped her eyes and looked out the side window. Could this man scar her any worse than Shane had? Then she had another surprise! Shane had never . . . Had never! *Had never!* The words reverberated in her head over and over, louder and louder. Shane had never affected her like this, not at all.

Because her face was turned away from him, Alan could read her expressions no longer, but he did wonder what was going on in that shrewd mind of hers. He could almost hear the cogs turning. He twisted the key, pressed the accelerator, and started the engine.

"Have I already begun to melt that frosty glaze around your heart, little Meg?" he quipped lightly, seriously wondering.

"Hardly," Megan retorted with a light laugh, her face swinging around. "I'm just hungry."

Before he began to drive away, he gave her another long, intensive stare. "I'm hungry, too, Megan. It's been a long, long time since I've had my hunger . . . satisfied."

Color rushed to Megan's face, but she refused to cower

before him. The only indication of her nervousness was the fidgeting of her hand on the collar of her blouse. She fingered the material agitatedly, and she chose to ignore his insinuations, accepting his remark at face value.

Alan chuckled, spinning the tires as he sped away from the house. "As I said, Megan, this evening is going to be pleasure-filled from start to finish."

"At least it's going to be action-packed," Megan quipped more seriously than jesting, wondering if she had made a mistake in coming.

As they drove to Del Rio, Alan surprised her by engaging in light banter, and when this died away naturally, he began to tell her about Matt's latest episodes, and both of them laughed. When the easy talk expired, he turned the radio on, and they listened to the music. During one of these moments of comfortable silence, Megan stared out the window at the shadowed scenery. She loved the rugged starkness of the landscape and marveled at its disturbing, unearthly beauty. She could understand why Joel felt such a compulsion to paint this land. He loved it, he felt it, and it was a vital part of him.

When they did reach the small border town, Alan meandered deftly through the streets until he reached an out of the way barbecue restaurant. He parked and switched off the ignition.

"Guaranteed to be casual, Megan," he teased with a wave of his hand.

Megan nodded her head, grinning, and as they walked into the barnlike structure, she couldn't have agreed more.

"I've always loved eating in a barn," she dryly retorted as the hostess led them through a maze of tables and benches into the back room.

"The food's terrific," Alan returned, swinging his long legs over the bench, "but it's the atmosphere that really grabs you."

Megan raised her brows quizzically, glancing around.

"What atmosphere?" she asked. "All that's missing is the cows." And she reached into the corner and pulled out a handful of hay. "They've even furnished us with hay."

Alan's fiery eyes spit flames of pure devilment, and his mouth moved in a mischievous grin. "That's what I'm talking about, Megan." His eyes swept up in the direction of the second floor. "After we've eaten we can take a tumble in the hayloft." A proud smirk creased his face. "Now, that's what I call an accommodating eating place."

"You'll take a tumble," Megan promised him, laughter in her eyes. "I'm going to take pleasure in knocking you off that pedestal of sheer male egotism that you're perched on."

"Many have tried, Meggie, and many have failed," he returned.

"I've never tried," she asserted with calm dignity, then added the promise, "and I don't fail."

The approach of the waitress stopped the flow of conversation, and as she placed two glasses of water on the table with the bowls of tossed salad, Megan studied the interior. The tables were made of rough lumber, and the decor was realistically reminiscent of a barn. The tablecloths were red-and-white checked, and the music definitely had the country-western flavor.

Alan pointed to the wall, which was covered by the menu written in large black letters. "What would you like to have?"

The waitress in full western regalia—a short denim skirt with imitation white leather fringe, white boots, white hat, and two monstrous pistols hanging on her hips—tapped her foot lightly against the plank floor and looked coquettishly at Alan. Even though the order pad was poised in her left hand, pencil in the right, she wasn't interested in taking the order too quickly.

Megan grinned when she had to repeat her order the second time, but she had to give it to Annie Oakley, once

64

she had taken their order she scurried away to return shortly with their food. The aroma of the hot barbecue wafted tantalizingly in the air, tempting Megan, reminding her poignantly of her hunger.

"I haven't had a bite to eat since breakfast," she remonstrated woefully, promptly filling her mouth with food. She chewed, savoring the delicious meal, and when she had swallowed her first mouthful, she said, "This is fantastic. Definitely worth our coming again."

So intent was she on eating that she didn't see Alan's head dart up at her pronouncement, nor did she see the smile of pleasure that danced across his face. Things were progressing smoothly, he thought. Megan was mellow and warm, although she was still slightly defensive, aggressively offensive. But, he smiled, he wouldn't have it any other way. He liked women with spirit.

As they ate, both were relaxed and in no hurry for the evening to end. Alan talked and Megan listened, asking a few questions now and then. By the time she had finished her meal, he was leaning back in the corner, one arm draped on the top railing of the bench, the other propped on the table. Because the dim light was on the wall behind and above his head, his face was shadowed, but Megan could tell that he was relaxed, and she thought she saw the slight smile that tugged those sensuous lips up.

He drained his mug, setting it down and wiping his mouth with the back of his hand. "Exactly what kind of work do you do, Megan?"

Sated, she leaned back herself against the hard straight railing, lifting her face, the soft light flickering over it, creating a total sexuality which appealed to Alan and whetted his sensual appetite. She shrugged and spoke modestly, but matter-of-factly and truthfully. "I'm the personnel director for Zelco."

He lifted his empty mug in the air, catching the attention of the waitress. "Hire and fire for the entire firm?"

"I'm in charge of taking applications and of testing and screening the applicants. If the applicant makes it past me, then he's ready for an interview with the individual department supervisor. Firing is left up to the individual supervisors."

"Like your work?"

"Love it," she murmured, sipping her tea. "I'm not tied to a desk, and I get to meet new people all the time." While he drank his second beer, she discussed her work, citing particular incidents that were unusually interesting or were comical.

"How do you like it out here?" he asked during a lull in the conversation.

Her eyes, which had been scanning the room absently, returned to his face. "This is my country," she declared, swirling the ice cubes in her glass. "Off and on I've thought about moving here, but the opportunity for a transfer has never occurred."

"You don't think you'd get tired of country living?"

"No," she returned with no hesitation.

"Continual isolation, simple country folk for neighbors, no social finery like you're accustomed to?"

She shook her head. "I wouldn't mind."

"Do you suddenly have a desire to bury yourself in the backwoods because you're running from unrequited love?"

Megan's head riveted upward, and she arched her brows. "What do you mean?"

"I mean you're here because you didn't want to face Shane. Don't you think you may have convinced yourself that you'd like to live here because you don't ever want to face him?"

Her voice was tinged with coolness when she answered him. She still resented his psychoanalyzing her. "I'm not afraid to face Shane," she admitted, wondering if that was the full truth or not. *I just wanted to meet him on my*

66

*terms, at my instigation,* she added to herself. Her eyes were remotely distant, the dreamy relaxation gone, the harshness of reality making them glitter with steely intensity. "I don't think you quite understand," she said with directness. "The only feeling I have for Shane is hatred. I hate him with an intensity that vibrates from my soul, a hate that equals the love I once had."

Alan shifted position effortlessly, loosening one of her hands from her glass, holding it in his, his fingers feather-touching the softness of her palm. How small, he thought, with an astounding hint of tenderness. Then he glanced at the set countenance, the narrowed lips, drawn in censure, the cold eyes.

"With so much hatred in your heart, Meggie," he crooned, "there can be no room for that love that someone wants to give you." The husky, vibrant tones were speaking in general, but the sensuality of the words were intimate and caressing.

Megan didn't succumb however. She just gave him a hollow smile that moved only her lips. "That's right," she intonated quietly but emphatically. "There's no room for love." His only response was a haughty lift of his thick russet brows.

Megan didn't like the erotic messages that his calloused hands were dispatching throughout her nervous system, and she didn't like his questioning her, hitting that one sensitive cord of her heart, gouging it, poking, twisting and turning. He made her feel vulnerable, giving her that helpless feeling again. She drew her hand from his with calculated movements—neither too fast nor too slow, but with methodical deliberation. She feigned indifference, not about to admit to him that she found his touch devastating. She had learned during the past eight months how to live—rather survive—behind this facade of indifference, and she wasn't going to help Alan in his storming of the Bastille.

She spoke when she saw the amused mockery that glared at her from those mute green eyes. "I really don't want love, Alan. I've found that I can live quite happily without it. I live for myself, and I have only myself to please."

Alan lifted the mug, drinking, staring over the rim of the thick glass at her. When he lowered it, he chided softly, "That's rather selfish." But his words were seasoned with a gentle tenderness that was Megan's undoing. "There's some fellow who would like to share his love with you."

Megan forced herself to laugh, but Alan knew that the causticity was deliberately injected. He could hear the brittle hurt that swayed underneath the weight of the sarcasm.

"Oh, yes," Megan murmured, "I understand sharing, Alan. The last two months that Shane and I went together, I shared him with Cardel Simmons, the woman who I thought was my best friend. It turned out that he preferred her to me." Her face was tight and uncompromising, her lips thinned with suppressed anger.

"Don't be so bitter. You've got to forget this guy and the way he's hurt you." Alan's eyes narrowed perceptibly, and he studied her. "Megan," he appealed softly, "don't you think maybe it's your pride that's hurt more than your heart?"

Megan felt the hysterical impulse to push her chair from the table and to run from Alan. How could he be so cruel, so crude, so blunt? If he wanted to take her to bed, this certainly wasn't a successful ploy, she exploded silently. But, again, she was forced to admit the truth of Alan's assertion. More than likely it was her pride more than her heart that had been hurt.

She took a deep breath, filling her lungs, exhaling slowly, composing herself. Then she shook her head, denying the truth. "No, you're wrong. He also broke my heart." She shrugged. "Perhaps my pride suffered, but my heart was broken in a million pieces"—her fingers bridged, and Alan saw her squeeze them until they were white—"a million little, tiny pieces."

"Forget him. Forget them. Forget the pain!"

She shook her head, her words and the movements equally vehement. "I don't want to forget. I want to remember." Following the slant of Alan's eyes, she looked at her hands. When she saw how tightly they were clenched together, she forced herself to relax. She lifted the pitcher of tea and poured herself another glass. "If you don't mind," she suggested as she dumped sugar into the glass and stirred, "I'd like to talk about something else. Talking about Shane and Cardel tends to ruin my evening."

After these curt words Alan easily swung the conversation into different channels, avidly describing his childhood in Dallas and his life since he'd been in Los Nogalitos. Carefully he avoided mention of his marriage, and although Megan noticed the omission, she didn't question him about it. He graphically relayed his disenchantment with his executive position with Glynn's Department Store and his leaving the large chain for the simple life of the dairy farmer. When he noticed her lids drooping, he smiled, grasping her hand in his, pulling her up.

"Come on, little girl," he teased, "it's time I got you home and put you to bed."

Megan grinned, comprehending his innuendo only too well. "You can take me home, but I'll put myself to bed."

With lithe economy of motion she walked to the truck with Alan, permitting him to hold her hand, but when he motioned for her to sit close to him in the truck on the ride home, she declined, shaking her head and scooting into the far corner. This was as close as she intended to get to him.

69

"Remember, I made no promises," she taunted, proud that she could prove to herself that she was capable of controlling her errant emotions. She wasn't a dittering female who could be swept off her feet by the forceful, undisguised lustfulness of Farmer McDonald.

"And you, remember, Megan Jonas—" The hushed words ominously drifted to Megan, their meaning almost a threat rather than a promise. "—I made no promises either."

Megan scrunched into a little ball, seeking comfort in her isolation, taking umbrage at his arrogant assertion. She said no more, nor did he as they drove through the sleepy little town. But once they were on the Interstate, clicking off the miles, Alan began to regale her with funny stories about himself and the farm, and Megan found herself listening, laughing, and relaxing. She was surprised when they bounced to a halt in front of the house.

Alan flicked off the headlights, pulled the key out of the ignition, and grabbed Megan's hand, pulling her across the seat before she could open her door and get out. He circled her waist with his arm, and when she tried to twist away, his fingers, five bands of iron, dug in. Demanding his pound of flesh, she thought ironically, as they walked across the lawn.

In the darkness, standing on the front porch, she fumbled through her purse for the key that still wasn't attached to a key chain. Finally tiring of the fruitless search, Alan jerked the purse from her and looked for the key himself.

"Is it on a ring?"

"No," she mumbled, "it's loose in one of the side pockets."

"You should put it on a ring," he grumbled, then added, "How come you keep so much junk in here?" not really wanting an answer.

At last he triumphantly lifted the small key, holding it

gingerly between thumb and index finger. He snapped her purse and crammed it into her hand while he fit the key into the lock, opened the door, and turned on the light. With quick movements he shoved the wooden door fully open but shut Bismarck behind the screen door, leaving Megan alone with him on the porch.

"I don't want that brute in the way tonight," he murmured, his eyes dancing with merriment. "He cramps my style." His back was to the light now, and he leaned against the screen, his face shadowed. Megan looked up at him, her face illuminated by the soft light that filtered through the thin mesh screen, fully understanding his declaration.

*Now for the payment,* she thought, mentally bracing herself for the final attack of the evening. Just one more skirmish, and she was home safe and sound . . . victorious. During the ride home she had allowed herself to give in to that hazy, carefree manner and had been lulled into a false sense of security. But now she tensed, dropping the relaxed easiness of the early evening.

"Thanks for the lovely evening, Alan," she said in a cool, even voice. "It's really been wonderful." But she knew the words were ineffective and were falling on deaf ears.

He arched his eyebrows, and Megan could feel the penetrating X ray of those eyes as they peered sardonically at and through her. "Oh, Megan," he mocked. "How polite! Surely I deserve more than this."

"Really," she intonated sarcastically. "What do you have in mind?"

"Let's say I'll settle for a kiss tonight, Megan. Later—" The velvet tones played with her nerves. "Later when you know me better, when you trust me, I'll tell you what I have in mind."

Megan forced herself to laugh with him, but she was frightened. She was standing too near him already. She could feel the warmness of his body, and hers longed, or, more aptly, it ached, ached badly, for his touch. She called on her reserve strength, remembering that to Alan this was no more than a game—a game of endurance, wits, and eventual submission, and she reminded herself that Alan planned to be the undisputed victor.

But, she also thought in that split-second, Alan had been truthful with her. He hadn't deceived her at all. He had announced his intentions, and he was following them through. Well planned and well executed! A good organizer!

Still she made no move to lessen the distance between them. Then his hand firmly gripped her wrist, gently tugging her closer. Each finger that circled her arm felt like a hot band of iron, searing and branding her flesh.

"I do want that kiss." The sound was silky-soft, smoothly gliding over her ragged nerves. "And I intend to take it."

One hand slid around her waist, clamping her to his body, arching hers more closely to him. The other cupped the back of her head, his fingers tangling in the soft spring curls, gently pulling her face closer and closer to his. His fingers closed on a handful of silken tresses, not roughly, but almost reverently, and he stopped the movement, looking into those gray eyes, so close, so wide, so apprehensive, luminous in the light that filtered through the screen.

She couldn't see his eyes, but she felt the small tongues of fire that leaped higher and higher, touching her, warming her, willing her to come to him. She had that giddy sensation in the pit of her stomach, the knot that grew larger and larger, tighter and tighter, the butterflies at the same time, and last—perhaps most important—she had the assurance that he was excited by her too. She felt the length of his body when it touched her shoulders, her midriff, lower—alerting her to his desire.

72

His head bowed, and just before she closed her eyes she saw those lips part—hard, firm, hot, moist, as they came toward hers. Demanding—not asking! They seduced her senses, seeking entrance for his tongue into the intimacy of her mouth.

She fought him, twisting and squirming, but his hand curled more firmly around the strands of her hair, stilling her movements, his lips exploring the goodness of her mouth, still arrogantly demanding more, his tongue teasing the cleft between the lips, but finding no opening in the gate of her mouth.

He lifted his mouth, not much, but enough to whisper on hers, the very movement sending tremors throughout her body. "No, Megan, I'm not going to settle for this." He stopped talking and nibbled on the fullness of her lower lip, each nip taking a larger bite into Megan's resistance. "If I'm not going to get you into bed with me tonight, I want a kiss, a proper kiss." Now he raised his head a little higher, his eyes soft and winsome, pleading. "Is that too much to ask?"

Intoxicated from his seduction, Megan shook her head, her lips saying no against his, but no sound came. And quickly she leaned on him, all resistance seeping out. Assured that he wasn't going to take her to bed, she ceased fighting. Her hands snaked around his neck, her fingers tangling in the thick waves at the nape of his neck. She lifted her face, offering her beautifully rounded lips for his pillage.

He lowered his, taking the offered territory, exploring once again, rediscovering the goodness . . . his tongue entering into that valley of sweet delight, eating his fill, exultant in his victory. His mouth moved over hers, pressing and gently tugging, teasing, giving, taking. He was arrogantly proud when she whimpered as he lifted his lips from hers, exhilarated when her hand cupped his head,

73

forcing his lips against hers. She began to take, to eat, to feast.

When she finally collapsed, totally drained of emotional energy, he lifted his lips, raining light kisses from her mouth down to her cheek, the slender column of her throat to the deep V of her blouse. He held her tightly, his lips again invading her privacy, again taking captive unclaimed territory, intent on capturing the prize.

His hand dropped down her back, blazing a hot trail wherever his fingers touched her, stopping only when they cupped the roundness of her buttocks. Just a little pressure from his hands, a slight movement of his hips, and Megan's hips began to arch toward him, an intense aching need building in the lower part of her body.

Losing herself in him, not caring for the moment if she ever found herself again, she pressed nearer and nearer to him, her breasts, tight and swollen, rubbing against the hardness of his chest. His hands, both in the small of her back, gently massaged, softly, tenderly, going round and round, each circular movement pulling the material of the blouse loose from the waistband of the skirt. She felt the warmth of the rough and calloused palms on her skin, and she wriggled closer, melding herself to him.

"Oh, God, Meggie," he breathed raggedly against her ears, "you're so good to hold, so wonderful to love. You feel so soft in my arms. I don't think I can let you go. I've waited so long for this, for you."

"Four days," Megan whispered incoherently, her reasoning in abeyance somewhere in that nebulous region called her mind. Right at the moment she didn't have time to be bothered with that. She was riding that crested wave of emotion, going higher, under the spray, catching her breath. Still she held on, refusing to give up this rapturous elation.

"No," he corrected her, "for the last five years. I've been waiting for you for five long years." But, even as he

74

talked, his hands wouldn't be stopped. She could feel the fiery soft touch as they caressed the smooth skin of her back, as his fingers strayed teasingly across her back under her arm, lightly moving toward her breasts. "Megan, let me make love to you."

Yes, her whetted senses clamored, and she nestled closer to his frame, inhaling his intoxicating, masculine scent, her face hiding on his firm chest. How nice it would be, she thought dreamily, to give in to these heady desires, to fulfill her body's needs, to assuage all these aches and wants. She sighed as his hands, his lips, his entire body joined in the sensuous assault.

"Come, Megan, let's go into the house."

The words jarred Megan, the movement startled her, and she bolted back to reality, almost nauseated at her sudden withdrawal from what she wanted so much.

"No," she whispered hoarsely, "no, I can't."

Her voice sounded guttural, too unreal to be her own. She realized that this was nothing but a conquest to Alan, a game to be won or lost, but it was her life. Then with a clarity that was crystal clear she knew: Her making love to him was a matter of her heart. She wasn't playing a game, she was responding to him. She wanted his touch, his caresses, his words of love and endearment. It would be too easy for her heart to become involved again.

"Megan." His words were faint. She had to strain to hear him, but they were reassuringly quiet. "I'm just as vulnerable this minute as you are. You're like a fine wine; you've gone to my head. I can drink and drink of your loveliness and beauty. Don't deny us this beautiful pleasure, sweetheart."

His words were as drugging as his lovemaking, and Megan could feel his persuasive magnetism. She wanted to give in, to let him take her to that glorious mountain of fulfillment, but she couldn't, not while it was a contest of wills—his against hers.

Sensing her submission, he maneuvered himself until he was leaning against the doorframe, and he pulled her closer to his arched body so that she could feel his pulsating hardness.

"See," he husked, "this is how much you're affecting me. It's not one-sided, Meg." His sigh was a purr of pleasure, his body quivering with desire.

"Any woman would do," Megan countered, taking several gulps of fresh air, willing herself to resist.

"No, that's where you're wrong," he said. "Only you." When she didn't speak again and when she made no further attempts to leave his arms, he said, "And I do the same to you."

These arrogant words injected spirit into her flagging resistance. How dare he, she thought angrily, whipping out of his arms. Not only was she angry with him, but more especially she was angry with herself because she allowed him the liberty of invading the privacy of her body, had flagrantly given him everything he wanted so far. But he wouldn't get more.

She smiled, her eyes now silvery slits, unreadable. Her voice was silky-smooth. "I think it's time for me to go in, and I know it's past time for you to leave."

Alan dropped his arms, staring at her face for a second, wondering where he'd gone wrong. She had been willing; she had wanted him. He would stake his life on it, but . . . Then with a hint of admiration he conceded. *She's a fighter. She's going to fight to the end.* And he was willing to wait until she gave in. There was no doubt in his mind that she would eventually surrender willingly.

He pulled on the screen door, letting her step into the house. Willing to give it another whirl, he said, "How about a cup of coffee?"

Megan chuckled softly, shaking her head. She pulled the door out of his unresisting hands, closed it, and snapped the latch into place. "Not tonight, Farmer. If you want coffee that badly, you go home and brew yourself a pot."

He grinned. "You're afraid, Megan. You're afraid if I come in, I'll get you in bed with me."

She smiled, feeling safer with the latched screen between them and with Bismarck between her feet. "You'll never know for sure, will you?" she taunted, her voice light and breathy, her eyes dancing with excitement, the taste of victory sweet in her mouth.

"I promise that if you'll make me some coffee, I won't go any further than you'll let me."

She shook her head. "No way."

She wasn't about to make that mistake, her eyes told him with sardonic mockery. She may have played the fool a minute ago in his arms, but she wasn't going to let him stay and seduce her in her own bedroom. An enigmatic smile flitted over her lips, darting to her eyes, where it lingered.

"I think, Alan, that you must concede victory to me," she announced with braggadocio. "Since I've been able to evade your magnetic charm, I think I've won the battle." To think, she reminded herself sweetly, although sharply, she had thought it would be a minor skirmish.

Alan's eyes danced with sheer delight and pleasure as they moved from Megan to Bismarck and back to her again. There she stood, her lips swollen and red, her hair loosened from the plastic clip, which lay on the porch somewhere discarded and forgotten about, her blouse rumpled and pulled out of the skirt band. Battle scarred, he thought, but proud and beautiful.

He folded his arms over his chest and rocked back and forth on his heels. "Yes, Meggie," he said thoughtfully.

"Yes, Meggie, what?" she goaded, not satisfied with his curt agreement.

"Yes, Meggie," he complied, "you've won this battle, but the war's far from being over." His words issued a challenge. "In fact," he pronounced with relish, his arrogance showing, "it's just begun."

He reached into his pocket and fished out his ring of keys, dangling them loosely in front of himself, looking for the right one. "Now, Megan, let's see how well you can do in the second battle."

"Which one?" she asked excitedly.

"How about spending the day with Matt and me tomorrow?" The question surprised him as much as it did Megan. It wasn't a habit of his to take women home for Matt to meet; this would be the first time.

She stood with her mouth open, almost shaking her head, wanting to nod, not quite knowing what to do. Did she dare spend a day in Alan's presence? Could she continue to resist him?

"I don't know," she evaded, stalling for time. She wanted to, but she didn't think it would be a wise choice.

"Matt will be very disappointed," he fabricated with no qualms. "I've told him about you and Bismarck." *And more about Bismarck than you,* he added silently.

Megan smiled, trying to still the erratic beating of her heart and the breathlessness she felt. This was the moment she'd been hinting for.

"I imagine he's more interested in the dog than in me."

"Perhaps," Alan conceded, his eyes warm, warm and beguiling with persuasive charm. "But if that's the case, you need to meet him to change his mind."

"Perhaps," she agreed softly, her lips curving in answer to his smile.

## CHAPTER FOUR

Megan woke early Thursday morning but didn't get up immediately. She lay in the gray stillness of the early morning, thinking about her day with Alan and Matt. It hadn't taken much persuasion, she reminded herself, for her to agree to go. Just the mention of Matt's name had been her justification.

She turned over, fluffing her pillow and twisting into a small ball. Was Matt the real reason she was going? Hardly, she answered, a beautiful smile playing around her lips. She was going because she wanted to be with Alan. She wanted to know as much about Alan as she could. She was going because she wanted to see this child who was part of the man who so intrigued her.

Yet Alan had known that she was on the brink of refusing. That's why he had used Matt's name. She smiled fully, flipping on her back, languorously stretching her willowy body under the clean white sheets. Alan wasn't all that sure about her, she thought. He believed he had her where he wanted her, but there was that tiny speck of doubt, just enough doubt to stand in good for Megan.

She wasn't worried about being with Alan today, however. She would have little Matt as chaperon, and there would be Rosa. At the thought of Rosa, Megan's smile widened mischievously. She rehearsed all the possible stories Elena might have concocted about her and wondered about Rosa's reception.

But Megan was a born optimist, and she refused to have her day ruined by what may or may not be. She took life as it came, the good with the bad, meeting it head-on and with a laugh most of the time. Her unhappy episode with Shane had probably been the most earth-shattering experience of her life, but she bounced back, quickly gaining her equilibrium, and she would be able to face him Monday with her dazzling smile—her new image.

She leisurely dressed and, since she had plenty of time, ate breakfast, then took Bismarck for a long walk. As the huge shepherd ran across the grassland, she walked behind, gazing at him with affection and pride. Since her parents had given him to her two years ago, the girl and dog had been inseparable.

After a long romp they settled down in the living room, Bismarck lying on the floor at her feet, Megan curled on the sofa with the latest biography of Napoleon in her lap. Although she was a history buff, she did little reading today; she had too much on her mind.

Daydreaming about her evening with Alan, she glued her eyes to the horizon and waited for the familiar truck. She even found herself wishing that she didn't have to return to Dallas at the end of the week. Oddly enough, this time her desire to remain in Los Nogalitos wasn't based entirely on her aversion to Shane. It had more to do with her attraction—her growing attraction—to Alan.

Her lips curved gently when she thought about the effect Alan was having on her, and she reasoned that it was good that she had found someone—a man—whom she could like and whom she enjoyed being with. And when he drove up much sooner than the appointed hour, Megan was still sitting on the couch, dreamy-eyed, her hand across the book. Soon the three of them—Alan, Bismarck, and Megan—were perched in the cab of the truck, headed toward Alan's farm.

"I think your dog is as suspect of my motives as you are," Alan teased, glancing at the animal that sat so arrogantly between the two of them, staring straight ahead, oblivious to both of them.

Megan looked over Bismarck's back to encounter that smile and the laughter that was mirrored in those emerald green eyes. She returned the smile, lifting a hand to lazily ruffle the fur around Bismarck's face. The raw desire shimmering in Alan's eyes had created a maelstrom of conflicting emotions and desires in her.

She turned her face, pressing it against the cool, smooth surface of the window, making a pretense of studying the countryside. If she could be one of those persons who enjoyed casual romances, she thought, she wouldn't feel like this. But she was different. She wanted more from life than a few nights with first this man and then that one. She wanted love, a love that brought with it happiness and warmth, a lover, a husband, a family.

That's why Shane's rejection had hurt her so badly. She had been under the impression that both of them had discovered their love together. When she learned differently, Megan swore never again to let her heart deceive her. Because she wouldn't compromise herself with fleeting romances, she had withdrawn from any kind of intimacy with a man. At best she would be friends, but she found that difficult. Men would say they would accept it, but before long they were asking or demanding more than she was willing to give.

Now Alan invaded that tender, badly scarred area known as her heart, and he walked heavily and cumbersome, unmindful of the half-healed places there. With each painful step of infringement, Megan felt in herself that same raw hunger that she saw reflected in his eyes. She had good reason to be leery of Alan McDonald, she thought, clenching her teeth together. If she weren't careful—very careful—she would give in to this man's demands.

Then she mentally shook herself, turning to look at him, trying to catch what he was saying. Because he was talking and looking at the road in front of the truck, Megan had the luxury of staring at him without any embarrassment. She could drink her fill of this rugged, primitive outbacker.

At the same time that this thought passed through her mind, Alan's head swept in her direction, and her cheeks turned a soft pink. Alan arched his brows and smiled, wondering what delicious secrets were flitting through her mind. He could see the happiness that spiraled from the center of her eyes, only slightly tinged with hesitancy.

She stared at him long after his eyes riveted back to the road. She had accused him of being unfeeling, but perhaps ruthless, overbearing, or arrogantly self-confident would be words which more aptly described him. She had the strong feeling that whatever he wanted he got, and he would probably have few scruples in obtaining it.

Almost before Megan was ready for it, Alan parked the truck in front of a large, rambling, white rock farmhouse with a red-tiled roof.

"Well, here it is. McDonald's Dairy Farm."

"It's beautiful," she murmured, loving the Mexican influence. "It fits the country."

Alan nodded his head, honking the horn until a small boy came running out of the house. Alan flung open his door and climbed out in time for the child, who was laughing and squealing, to throw himself into his father's arms. Alan swung Matt into the air.

"Here we are," he announced amid the giggles and screeches.

"I've been waiting," Matt panted in between giggles. "I didn't think you'd ever get here. Did you bring her with you?" He squinted into the truck and saw first Bismarck, then Megan. Thrusting the unruly shock of jet black hair out of his dark eyes, he smiled tentatively at Megan.

Then she heard the subdued "Hi."

Megan smiled, instantly captured by the beauty of the brown eyes. "Hello, Matthew. How are you?"

She opened the door, swinging her feet to the ground. She walked around the truck to stand close to father and son.

Matt squirmed from his father's arms. "I'm okay. My name is Matt."

Megan squatted beside him. "Glad to meet you, Matt. You can call me Meg—or Megan. I answer to both." She held her hand out, and Matt placed his small one in hers.

"What's your dog's name?"

"This is Bismarck," she answered as the dog sauntered up, sitting beside her. "Bismarck, this is Matt. Shake hands with him." The dog extended his right paw and barked at the same time.

Matt squealed with delight, reaching out to take Bismarck's paw. "I like you Big Mark." And "Big Mark" seemed to like Matt too.

Megan stood in time to see an older woman walk out of the house with Elena. Elena, ignoring Megan, ran to Alan, putting her hand on his forearm. The older woman, a smile stretched across her face, walked toward Megan, warmth and friendliness shining in her dark eyes.

Out of the corner of her eye Megan watched as Elena monopolized Alan, but she also tried to concentrate on Rosa's introduction.

"And you must be Megan? Joel has told us so much about you."

Megan smiled. "Yes, I'm Megan, and you must be

Rosa." She chuckled. "Alan's told me so much about you."

Rosa joined Megan in her laughter, her voice soft and husky. "I'm glad that you're spending the day with us. Matt and I have been looking forward to meeting you." When she spoke again her voice carried a soft reprimand. "We were worried about your staying at Joel's by yourself, and we were hurt because you didn't come stay with us."

Then Elena's shrill voice interrupted the soft drone of Rosa's. "But, Alan, remember you promised to pick me up after work this afternoon."

Rosa's brows furrowed in consternation, and she answered before Alan could speak. "I've already told you that I'd pick you up, Elena."

Megan watched in fascination as Elena's fingers caressed Alan's arms and as she disregarded her mother's words. She spoke, her voice now low and husky like her mother's. "You promised, Alan, and I've made plans for us tonight."

Alan caught her hands in one of his and stopped the intimate teasing. "I told you that I'd pick you up if your mother couldn't, but I didn't promise to go out with you and your friends." He grinned. "Why don't you take the car?"

Pouting, Elena jerked her hand out of his and flounced off in a huff. "I don't want to take the car, but don't either of you bother about coming to pick me up. I'll get someone to bring me home." She strutted by Megan, never speaking. "I'll wait for Darren out here."

Rosa, embarrassed over her daughter's behavior, but indulgent, chose to ignore Elena's outburst and rudeness, speaking to Megan in order to cover the tension. "Come on, Megan, we'll go inside and visit."

Alan and Megan followed her, but Matt and Bismarck went scampering across the lawn. Alan's hand, gently prodding her in the middle of her back, guided her up the stone walkway. Although his fingers barely touched the material, much less her flesh, she felt as if it were a tongue of fire burning into her skin. Her first impulse was to shake herself free from him, but she didn't want him to know how much he was affecting her.

Alan suddenly chuckled, and Megan thought he had read her thoughts. "Well, Meggie," he said, pushing on the large Spanish-styled door, "looks like I don't have to worry about handling the beast before I handle the beauty."

Not following the gist of his remark, she suspiciously lifted her face, looking up at him questioningly. "I don't understand," she said.

"Looks like my son is going to help his old man out. While he distracts, er, *entertains* Bismarck, I'll entertain the maiden. How do you like that?"

Megan chuckled with him, glad that he couldn't read her mind. "I'll take my chances," she retorted bravely, knowing she'd be going home in the morning and would probably never see him again.

With a slight nudge and another chuckle Alan prodded her into the foyer of the house, which was welcoming with its quiet coolness. She immediately felt an affinity with the white stucco interior and the *saltillo* tile floors. Turning immediately to the left, she moved into a spacious living room which was recessed several feet, its masculine elegance catching her attention—the carpet was of different brown tones, the walls were painted an off-white, the decor was Mexican, and the furniture heavy and ornate, but highly functional.

At the end of the living room nearest to the foyer was the formal dining area, which was elevated, and was separated from the living area with a black wrought iron railing. Next to the dining area, also elevated, was a roomy kitchen and breakfast nook which opened into the laundry room. The breakfast area was accessible through a door which was in the far end of the living room. Thus the house offered privacy and openness at the same time.

Sitting in one of the massive armchairs, his feet resting on an ottoman, crossed at the ankles, Alan asked, "Well, what do you think?"

She sat on the edge of the sofa, still admiring the beauty of the house. "It's beautiful. I never dreamed that it would look like this." She grinned. "I guess I expected a house similar to Gramps's. Did you renovate it yourself?"

Shaking his head, he answered slowly, his eyes roaming around the room. "I had it renovated when Linda was pregnant with Matt. She and I were going to live here." He smiled whimsically. "This was probably one of the few times that we did something together that both of us enjoyed." Reminiscing, he said, "She loved restoring old things. Her dream was to completely restore the Hacienda Del Lago, but this was all that we got around to doing." He flashed her that winning, lopsided smile. "But someday I'll get it finished."

Megan had no time to pose any more questions because Matt opened the door at that time and, followed by Bismarck, skipped down the steps into the room. "Daddy, what are we going to do today?"

Alan picked the boy up and set him on the arm of the chair. "I don't have any plans. I thought we'd let the day take care of itself. What would you like to do?"

"Let's go to the lake and have a picnic!" His eyes were bright and shining with anticipation. "I'd like to take Big Mark." He glanced around. "And I'd like to take Megan too."

Alan looked at Megan, a smile tugging his lips, his eyebrows arching. She read the question and answered. "I'd love to go on a picnic, Matt. Although I've seen the lake many times, I've never been there with anyone else but Gramps. And I'm sure Bismarck would like a picnic too."

"Can we, Daddy? Please, can we?"

Megan smiled, watching the small boy manipulate the man so cleverly. With mock seriousness, Alan answered, "I don't know, Matt. What if Rosa doesn't feel like making us a lunch?"

"I'll make it then," Matt shouted.

Alan threw his head back and laughed, a deep, resonant sound.

"I'm sure you would. It just so happens that I don't like peanut-butter-and-jelly sandwiches."

Matt looked crestfallen, then he revealed joyously, "Megan can make your sandwiches, Daddy, and I'll make mine."

"Now, that's an idea," Alan agreed, darting Megan a surreptitious look, "but should we make our guest work in order to go on our picnic?"

"Please, Daddy," the child pleaded.

"What do you say, Megan?" Alan asked, standing to his feet, Matt swinging from his hands as if they were a maypole.

"I'm in favor," she retorted smugly, winking at Matt. "And I'll even volunteer to make the sandwiches."

In mock exasperation Alan shrugged his shoulders. "Well, it looks like I'm outnumbered. Guess we'll have to check with Rosa to see if we've got the makings for a picnic."

Having overheard their conversation, Rosa called from the kitchen. "We've got the makings all right, but remember Matt's got to go to the doctor for his shots this afternoon."

"Aww, Buella," Matt groaned. "Take me some other time." And he scampered into the kitchen to try his wiles on Rosa.

Following at a slower pace were Alan and Megan. "Can't do that, Matt," Alan negated firmly.

Alan and Megan stepped into the kitchen as Rosa said,

"Your father's right, Matt. You've got to get those shots today." She looked down at the drooping head and listened with patient amusement at his dejected sigh. "But you've got time for a short picnic. How's that?"

Matt's head swung up, and his mouth opened into a wide circle of happiness. "We can go, Buella? We can go?"

Alan opened the refrigerator door, taking out a large roast. "Here, I'll slice this, and you and Megan can make the sandwiches." He moved toward the butcher block in the center of the room.

"Megan can make the sandwiches," Rosa corrected, opening the pantry door, handing Megan the mayonnaise and mustard. "I'll pour the tea, and, Matt, you can make your own sandwiches, but be sure to put the peanut butter and jelly away when you're through." She filled the container with tea. "Megan, you'll find the tomatoes and lettuce in the vegetable crisper."

"I'll get them," Matt sang as he danced toward the refrigerator.

Rosa walked back to the pantry, bringing out a large picnic basket. She lined it with a square of white linen and as soon as Megan had made the sandwiches, she put them in. "I'll be out to pick Matt up about two, Alan. That will still give me time to get him in for his appointment. By the way," Rosa added, pointing to the message tablet by the phone, "don't forget the agent from the milk association who's coming this afternoon."

Alan nodded his head, putting the container of iced tea in the basket and covering it with a tablecloth. "I'd forgotten about it already." He looked down at Matt, who was liberally spreading the peanut butter and jelly over a slice of bread. "Well, partner, I guess both of us are destined to having half a picnic today." Then he lifted his eyes and caught Megan's. He smiled. "But I suppose half a picnic is better than none at all, isn't it?"

"Yes," Matt muttered, the tip of his tongue jutting

slightly from the corner of his mouth as he concentrated on getting the thick brown spread from the jar to the bread. "But I wish I didn't have to go to the doctor."

"Me, too, but that's the way it is," Alan returned, looking from Rosa to Megan when he asked, "Are we ready?" Both women nodded. "I'd like to stay longer myself, but I can't either." He swung the basket over his arm and walked behind Megan, again placing the fingers of his free hand lightly in the middle of her upper back, guiding her to the door. "We'll just have to plan another picnic real soon."

With hasty good-byes and last-minute instructions, it was a few minutes before they were on their way, but soon the truck was disappearing in the distance, Matt and Bismarck in the bed, while Alan and Megan sat in the front. Rosa stood at the front gate, waving until she could no longer see the little hand flying in the air.

Alan kept Megan laughing as the truck bounced and jostled over the narrow dirt road, surprising her when they reached the cluster of scrub oaks that sheltered a small, clear lake—El Lago Lindo—the pretty lake. Megan never tired of looking at the lake, and she loved the quiescent beauty of the spot. It was her hideaway. During the many summers that Gramps had brought her out here, she had always found a retreat, almost a haven, in this small lake.

And Joel had promised Megan many years ago that he would never sell this particular spot. It was hers. "I love this place," she breathed. "It's lovelier than I had remembered."

Jumping in the back of the truck, Matt cried excitedly, "Do you like it, Megan?"

"Love it," she sang back, her happiness bubbling over also.

"Can I go swimming, Daddy?" Matt asked as Alan switched off the ignition.

"I suppose you can," Alan returned, swinging open his door. "Did you bring your trunks?"

"Sure did," Matt grunted, leaning over to pick up a small square of red cloth. He ran to the other side of the truck, leaned forward, and called into the open window. "Are you going to swim, Megan?"

"Not today," she returned, lazily scooting down in the seat, in no hurry to get out. "I didn't bring my bathing suit with me."

"Don't go into the water until I get there," Alan instructed as Matt hastily wiggled out of his clothes into the suit.

"Okay," Matt answered, jumping over the side of the truck, scampering away with the dog. "We'll just explore for a little while."

Alan held his hand across the seat, motioning for Megan to slide over. She, however, stared at his hand for a long time, then looked up and smiled, a wary remoteness in her eyes. As quickly, the distant aloofness was replaced with a devilish gleam. She wasn't afraid of him today—the sun was shining, it was broad daylight, and there was Matt. Why not push Alan as far as she could? He couldn't retaliate until it was too late.

A warmth slowly infused the smile, wiping out all traces of the icy blue veil that had shrouded her. With that motionless grace, she lifted her arm, her soft hand falling into his. But she didn't move until he gently tugged.

"Ah, Meggie," he breathed, his eyes almost belching smoke and ashes, "you're going to get burned again if you don't stop playing with fire."

The musical tones of her laughter were quietly evocative. "I didn't realize that I was playing with fire," she fabricated teasingly. "I certainly wouldn't do it intentionally."

"Liar," Alan charged softly, not disturbing the hushed

90

stillness. "You're enjoying every minute of this emotional seduction."

Again Megan laughed, the realization that she hadn't laughed so much in months racing through her finely tuned awareness. "Am I seducing you?" she coquettishly inquired, tilting her head slightly to the side, lowering her thick lashes, fanning them against the delicate pink of her cheeks.

Before she knew it, Alan slid into the truck and his fist was resting beneath her chin, gently lifting her face. "It's a good thing we've got a chaperon, little Megan," he assured her, holding up the gauntlet, letting her know that he hadn't thrown it down again. "If we didn't, I'd make you rue the day you set out to play with Alan McDonald."

Again those euphonious strands of laughter touched his ears, filling him with a drugged languor. "That's unfair of you, Farmer McDonald," she chided in soft tones. He lifted that haughty, russet brow queryingly. Her gray eyes were alive, vibrant with challenge. "Surely you of all people should know what's good for the goose is good for the gander."

His head lowered, a deliberate frontal attack, and his hand splayed, the fingers now firmly cupping the chin, holding her face in position. His eyes, a blazing forest green, didn't ask; they didn't question; rather they arrogantly assumed, blatantly demanded her response.

Waiting, she didn't move a muscle, watching as he slowly moved in closer, the clean masculine smell a narcotic to her nerves, his warm breath faintly whispering against her mouth and her chin. His lips, full, firm, moistly rich, were poised just a breath away, almost touching, not quite. Hers pouted, inviting, inticing him.

But just as he leaned over to capture his prize, Megan quickly averted her face and pulled back, laughing softly and breathlessly. Almost, she thought, taking a deep gulp of air, almost she hadn't withdrawn. Almost she had given in to that heady desire and those amorous poundings of her heart.

Alan's mouth curved into a tight smile, but he wasn't pleased with Megan's teasing. Always in the past he had been the one who did the teasing, the one who led the affair on, and he didn't like having to wear the other shoes.

"Just wait, Megan," he promised tightly. "There'll come another day."

Megan didn't have time to retort because Matt cried impatiently from the bank of the lake.

"Daddy, come on. I want to go swimming."

"Saved this time, Megan," Alan muttered huskily, "but there will be another." He turned his head and answered Matt. "I'm coming, Matt. Let me get the basket." His hand closed over hers, and he pulled Megan across the seat. "We'll have to save this little skirmish until later, Meggie. My son seems to be getting impatient, and he doesn't have too long to swim before Rosa will pick him up."

They scooted out of the truck, Alan stopping long enough to scoop the picnic basket from the back. Carrying it under one arm, he caught Megan's hand in the other, and they walked toward the edge of the lake hand in hand.

Matt looked up at them, his face screwed against the glare of the noonday sun, his toes in the lucid blue water of the lake. "Is she your girl friend?"

Alan dropped the basket. "Yeah, I guess you'd call her that," he answered lazily, an enigmatic expression in his eyes. "Is that okay?"

Matt didn't answer. He looked first at his father, then at Megan. Slowly that lopsided grin so like Alan's swept across his little face. "Yep," he mumbled, kicking a pebble, his gaze never leaving Megan's. He looped an arm around Bismarck's neck. "I like Big Mark." Peeking from behind the broad shoulders of the dog, he asked, "Are you going to marry her?"

Megan's face registered surprise, but she only looked from Matt to Alan, who was winking and grinning broadly at her. "Well, I've got something like that in mind, Matt, but I'm not sure about Megan. I'll have to talk it over with her. What do you think about the idea?"

"It's okay," Matt mumbled again. "Can we keep Buella, too?" But he didn't wait for an answer. He turned suddenly and ran toward the water, calling over his shoulder, "Can I swim now?"

Alan nodded, easing his large frame down beneath the shady umbrella of the trees. He patted an area close to him. "Come sit down, Megan. Let's get better acquainted with each other." He grinned at her affronted expression, almost reading the venomous thoughts that were ricocheting in her brain. His eyes, green as the spring foliage on the trees above and as bright and crisp as the grass below, rollicked with amusement.

"I love the way you propose, Farmer McDonald," she finally spit dryly, not budging from her spot. "I suppose all farmers carry on their romances like this."

Alan's eyes were on the boy now. "No farther, Matt," he yelled. "That's far enough." Then he lay back, crossing his hands under his head, but Megan saw his lips twitch into that infernal one-sided grin, and she heard the mockery in his voice.

"I'm not really sure how other farmers court their women, Miss Jonas." His head tilted slightly to the side. "You see, I've never courted since I've been a farmer," he added with a chuckle. "This is my first experience."

Megan sat down, leaning against the trunk of the large tree, putting space between her and Alan. "I think perhaps you need some practice," she quipped lightly, keeping her eyes on Matt and Bismarck. "You're rather clumsy and inept."

"Reckon I am," he drawled in that slow south Texas

93

vernacular. "I don't make it a habit to propose too frequently. So far this has only been my second time."

Megan giggled. "I guess Matt thinks you're going to marry each woman that you bring home for him to meet?" She wasn't above ferreting out information in any way she could.

Alan rolled over, bringing himself closer to her. Chewing on a blade of grass, he replied, "Wouldn't know. You're the first one I've brought home for him to meet." Megan's face flamed with color, but she said nothing. "What, Miss Jonas," he ribbed, "no fancy retort? No way to put the simple farmer down? Can't think of anything to say?" When Megan didn't reply, he said softly, "Don't soften up, little hellcat. I probably wouldn't know how to react, and I may do something that you wouldn't like."

Megan's eyes, as if riveted to a magnet and with no control of their own, lost the image of the boy and dog, locking on the full rugged handsomeness of Alan McDonald's face. If she had tried, she couldn't have broken away from those eyes. Glowing deep in their depths were the red-hot embers of reckless desire mingled with a warm tenderness.

Megan knew she was out of her depth. Never in her life had she experienced emotional bottomlessness as she did now. She wanted to reach out to grab something, to hang on, so she wouldn't drown in this swirling whirlpool. What kind of game was he playing? Why had he told Matt that?

"I—I—" She tore her eyes from his. She couldn't think and have him stare at her like that. "I don't appreciate your idea of a joke," she finally mumbled, unable to be assertive, but still fighting to master her errant senses and reason.

"No joke," he explained. "I'm serious." His fingers tapped her chin, the slight pressure guiding her face back to his. "I want you to marry me."

"Marry you!" she echoed incredulously. "Marry you!"

"You don't have to give me your answer now," Alan said, disregarding her shocked outburst. "I just wanted you to start thinking about it."

"I don't have to think about it," Megan blurted. "The answer is a flat no. I don't know you, and you don't know me. Why could you possibly want to marry me? Why should I want to marry you?" She didn't even pause for an answer. "No. The answer is no. I don't want to marry you. I don't want to marry anybody."

"Okay," Alan returned indifferently, removing his hand from her chin and lying down again. "That's that." He chewed on the blade of grass for a minute, giving her time to compose herself. "What do you think of this beautiful lake that the Spanish missionaries so aptly named?"

Megan gaped at him. He was an enigma she'd never understand. In a casual, joking way he tells his son that he wants to marry her and when she calls him to task about it, he proposes. And when she turns him down, he just as coolly turns away from the subject and begins to talk about some mundane subject like the weather.

Never, she thought heatedly, never had she met anyone like Alan McDonald before. She nervously squirmed around, trying to find a comfortable sitting position, one that didn't throw her so close to him. She wasn't capable of thinking straight when she was touching him, and the way he was acting, she needed to be on her guard at all times.

He threw the blade of grass down and swerved his head to the side, looking at her, watching her twist this way and that way. "I said, what do you think of the lake?"

"It's beautiful," she returned, her voice sounding cool and serene. "I've always loved it, and I'm glad that Gramps is going to let me have it." Then and only then did she look directly into his face. "Gramps promised me."

"For a place you claim to love so much, you've certainly stayed away for a long time."

Megan nodded. "I know." She shrugged. "I just got caught up in earning a living . . . and other things."

"And mostly other things," Alan added. When she turned her venomous gaze on him, he laughed. "But that's not bad, Megan. It's just a fact of life."

"I guess so," she admitted quietly.

"What would you do with this if Joel gave it to you?"

She lay beside him, not touching him, looking up at the beautiful blue sky that was draped with the large voluminous white clouds. "I want to build a home here, but I don't want to ruin the natural beauty of the land." She paused. "Whatever I build will have to complement the surroundings."

"Matt, come back in," Alan yelled before he said to Megan, "What kind of house do you have in mind?"

She was still staring at the sky. "It would have to be Spanish in design." She turned her head, eyeing him. "You know what I mean?"

"Um-hmm," he droned lazily, closing his eyes against the warmth of the sun.

"Adobe or white stucco with the red-tile roof." Slightly chagrined at herself for admitting to this dream, she said, "You think I'm silly, don't you?"

"No," he reassured her, cocking open one eye, looking about for Matt. "I don't think it's silly." His hand closed over hers. "And even if I did, there have been others who didn't think it was so silly."

"Oh?" she questioned, her brows arching.

"Sometime during the early 1700s Don Pedro Fernando de Vasco y Maria Mateo Mendoza was given a large land grant by the king of Spain, and somewhere in the vicinity of El Lago Lindo he built a beautiful hacienda."

"What happened to it?"

"Among other things, Indian uprisings," Alan returned. "The hacienda was totally destroyed. Not a trace of it remains. Little by little the land was sold until nothing of the original land grant was left."

"It would be wonderful if someone could get it all together again, wouldn't it?"

"Someone is," he replied. "Me."

Megan flipped to her side, resting her head on her propped arm. "How many acres were in the original grant?"

"One thousand, of which I own all but the last hundred."

"And part of that hundred is this property around the lake," Megan supplied.

Alan grinned, his expression totally lackadaisical. "You're right."

"And I can promise you that you won't get it from Gramps," Megan gloated. "He's promised it to me."

"Even if he could get more than the property was worth?" Alan questioned. "You know he's not getting any younger, and he needs to prepare for his retirement."

Megan giggled. "What retirement! Gramps won't ever quit painting, and his reputation is well established. He doesn't need your money. Besides," she added, "he's promised it to me."

"You'd hold him to that promise when you haven't been out here in six or seven years?"

"Why not?" she quipped lightly, not liking this gentle reprimand by Alan.

He shrugged his shoulders and replied indifferently, "Why not?"

"Is this your dream, Alan?" Megan demanded on a quizzical note. "To buy all the land that was in the original land grant?"

"I don't have time for dreams," he replied bluntly, almost curtly. "But, yes, Megan, I do want to buy the property, and there's nothing I would like better than to restore the hacienda to its former glory."

"Restore," Megan scoffed. "You mean rebuild." She squinted her eyes against the glare of the afternoon sun. "It certainly sounds like a dream to me."

Alan's eyes opened wide, the lucid green spheres staring into her face. "It's more a goal than a dream, Megan," he corrected her. "One that I shall attain. I promise you."

"Is that your only . . . as you say, goal?" Megan quizzed.

"No, that's not my only goal. I intend to marry you." Amorous fires flashed in the forest green of his eyes.

"I doubt it," Megan returned sarcastically, her nerves tingling from his emotional caress.

"I don't, but we'll not talk about it right now."

Very adroitly he changed the subject, and he and Megan lay underneath the trees talking, while Bismarck and Matt played in the water. Alan kept his eyes on the youngster, and he talked about his plans and hopes for the dairy farm. Finally he glanced at his watch.

"Soon be time for Rosa, then it'll be time for me to meet with Fitzgerald from the association." He levered up, calling to Matt. "Come eat. It's about time for Buella."

Matt came splashing out of the water, running to Alan, who pointed in the direction of the truck. "Your towel and dry clothes are in the front seat. Dry off and change in the truck." Matt danced off as Alan reminded him, "Make sure you get your boots on the right feet." Matt giggled, slamming the truck door.

While he changed, Megan spread the lunch, and when he returned, the three were ready to delve into the sandwiches and chips. For a short period they abandoned all talk and entertainment for the sheer pleasure of appeasing their appetites. By the time Rosa drove up, they had finished their meal and were sitting around laughing and talking.

Alan walked Matt to the car, opened the door, and

leaned over, talking to Rosa. As he did this, Megan gathered the remains of the lunch, stuffing it into the basket. When she had cleared up, she lay back on the thick carpet of grass, bunching the tablecloth to pillow her head. She was lying on her back, one hand under her head, the other lying across her stomach, when Alan returned.

"Don't we look comfy," he teased, easing down beside her.

Rolling to the side, putting some distance between them, Megan replied torpidly, gazing limpidly at him, "I'm feeling rather lazy at the moment."

He stretched his legs and leaned on one elbow, using his free hand to trace the outline of her eyebrows. "You look rather kissable right now." His face lowered, his lips tantalizingly close, but not close enough. His breath fanned her cheeks, whispering across them, teasing the short tendrils of hair. When he saw the raw hunger shimmering in her eyes, he teased her even more.

"I'm afraid that you'll withdraw again, Megan."

"I might," she whispered, giving voice to a lie, her lips lightly touching his with tormenting sweetness.

"Say please," he enjoined softly. "Say please, and I'll kiss you."

"I don't beg," she whispered back, her hand catching the back of his head, pulling it down so that his mouth covered hers.

At the moment she gave no thought to the future, nor did she worry about her traitorous feelings. She wanted his nearness, his caresses, as much as he wanted to give them to her. That aching void needed fulfillment, and her body screamed for just the touch of Alan's hands, his mouth, his arms.

Alan, sensing her surrender, let the kiss deepen, his tongue prising between the full softness of her lips, moving into the moist richness of the cavity below, her tongue caressive in its greeting to his. With a low groan his body lowered, pressing onto hers, and her other arm wound around his neck.

When he lifted his face, his lips made a moist path from her mouth to the arched column of her throat, his tongue chasing chills down the side of her neck to that soft sensitive hollow at her shoulder.

"Megan, will you marry me?" The words were romantic, soft, cajoling, and, she thought in hazy surprise, he's earnest! He isn't joking. "Please, Meggie."

Her eyes were dark, gun-metal gray, glazed with desire, tinged with confusion and uncertainty. She couldn't understand why Alan would come on so strong for marriage so quickly. Her hand rested on his cheek, her fingers of their own volition lightly feathering the chiseled handsomeness.

"Is this part of the game?" she whispered, wondering if he'd use tactics like this.

He shook his head. "No, Meggie, it's not part of a game. I'm too old for games. I'm fighting for my happiness."

She dropped her hand and turned her face from his. "And marriage to me will make you happy?"

"Yes," he returned, his lips nibbling the exposed neck and ear.

"I don't know." Her words were breathy, quivering with hesitant indecision. "I just don't know, Alan." She paused, drew in a lungful of air, and asked, "Why marriage, Alan?"

"You'd rather I'd suggest an affair?" he countered evasively.

"No," she grated with a grimace, "that's not what I meant. I want to know why you so suddenly sprang this on me."

"It's not sudden," he contradicted, his voice deep and resonant, low and seductive, his lips brushing the sensitive area behind her ears, his tongue intimately exploring the tender outer ear.

"Don't," she murmured, squirming against his muscular frame, twisting her head, tantalizing sparks dancing over her body.

Her words, however, were lost under the touch of his firm, moist lips. Though she struggled against him, though she denied even to herself that she would surrender, she knew that she was quickly losing not only the battle but the war. His touch was her undoing.

Sinking into the abyss of swirling emotion, casting reason aside, Megan joined Alan in the quest for fulfillment. As he explored the goodness and sweetness of her body, she did the same with his.

Her hand cupped the back of his head, her fingers splaying through the thick rusty locks, the tips massaging the scalp. When he finally raised his head to look into her eyes, a soft sound escaped her lips, and her fingers trailed paths of fire down his cheeks.

Her eyes, heavy and languorously glazed with desire, shimmered like melted glass, their crystalline beauty drawing a soft sigh from him as his head dropped again, his lips finding the swelling flesh of her breasts which escaped the scooped neck of her knit shirt. She felt the full force of that hard, seeking mouth, the warmness and the wetness as his tongue tormented her with tiny, hot, licking flames until she was ablaze like a raging fire.

Then his mouth was on hers again, and she was suffocated with his nearness, his taste, his smell, his feel. The tangy aftershave drifted into her nostrils, his clean masculine smell, the crisp, spring smell around them. Her lips parted—inviting first, accepting next—the driving exploration of his tongue.

Her body twisted, and she welcomed . . . she craved . . . the hardness of his body against hers. In response he turned, one hand cupping her hips, drawing them closer to him, his mouth still on hers, his tongue still probing the velvet splendor of hers. He pressed her hips to his, pressed her into his burgeoning masculinity. Convulsively she shuddered and would have withdrawn her mouth to hide her face in his shoulder, but he refused the request.

Still he was gentle; still he was tender; yet his lovemaking was forceful and determined. His passion had mounted to a point that was almost overwhelming, making him poignantly aware of his needs, but his experience, his expertise, alerted him to her hunger, her needs, their mutual desires, allowing him the initiative, delegating him the responsibility.

Fully responding, totally following the lead, she wrapped her arms around his shoulders, her fingers gripping into the flexed muscles of his back. Her mouth savored the delicious warmth of his, her tongue engaging in the duel, stroking, withdrawing, entering again. Her mind had ceased to work, and she reveled in the abandoned, thoroughly wanton pleasure they were giving to each other.

Now she felt those rough hands, gentle and tender, as they slipped under the knit shirt, capping the swollen breast, his thumb and index finger rolling the peaked nipple softly. Evocatively she writhed, moving closer to him, and her lips moved, a tiny moan escaping.

She began to resist, desperately gathering her shattered —or was it her scattered—wits about her. How could she let him take her like this? How could she comply so easily?

"No," she murmured thickly, "I can't—I—don't do this."

The emerald eyes gazed into her face, deep green, thoroughly washed with longing and desire, glinting with purpose.

"Sweetheart," he breathed, his lips descending once again on her mouth, "you know it's inevitable. It's going to happen."

And she did know!

The knit shirt was up, and he bent his head to caress the

naked throbbing peaks of her breasts, his tongue a flaming torch, sending shivers of fire throughout every cell of her body, igniting a burning sensation in the core of her body, a painful burning.

Her fingers clumsily unbuttoned his shirt, and her hand brushed across his hair-rough chest. She thrilled when she felt his body quiver; she rejoiced when she felt the thundering of his heart; she melded herself closer when she heard his ragged, uneven breathing.

Drowning in that sweet, priceless wine of his passion, intoxicated by his drugging kisses, Megan pressed her head closer until his teeth gently nipped the satiny skin in the curve of her neck and shoulder. Then her hand clasped his head, guiding his mouth back to hers. She must have it; without his lips she was naked and undone.

Unable to relinquish her mouth also, he lifted his lips slightly, his words a breathy whisper. "I think you must concede victory to me, sweet." His hand now rested under the waistband of her jeans, his fingers splaying against the smooth skin of her stomach, the tips resting on the elastic of her bikini panties, erotic tremors shaking her slender form.

Perhaps it was the gentleness of his tone, perhaps it was the emotional high of the moment, she wasn't sure, but finally the words registered. Shock registered! It was as if her blood stopped coursing through her body; her breath caught in her throat. She remembered!

This was nothing more than a game—a dare. She could still hear those words "Winner takes all!" A dumb, stupid game, she cursed, tears swimming in her eyes, and she'd almost given in, almost let him love her.

Taking a deep breath, slaking the horrible constriction in her chest, she turned her face from him, pressed her palms against the naked chest, and shoved herself out of his arms. "I—I don't think so," she sputtered on a gasp, squirming into a sitting position, raking her fingers through her disheveled hair, yanking her shirt down at the same time.

"And what does this mean?" he thundered, his face cloudy with raw hunger, his eyes shimmering with unfulfilled needs.

"I mean I don't want you to make love to me," she cried.

He emitted a bitter growl. "You're lying through your teeth. What made you suddenly change your mind?"

Megan rolled over, putting some distance between the two of them. "I don't like the idea of your playing with my emotions."

"My God," he exploded, "you were wreaking havoc with mine. How can you get this far and call it quits just like this?" He snapped his fingers together. "My guts are twisted together in a knot, and I'm nauseated with wanting." His fingers swiftly buttoned his shirt. "If I wanted to play, lady, I'd certainly pick a different game. When it comes to love, I'm absolutely serious."

Megan could hear the ragged anguish in his voice. She could feel the same knot in her stomach, the aching void deep within. Yet she refused to acknowledge it.

"I want to know why you suddenly decided to propose," she said, breathing sharply, her hand unconsciously rubbing her stomach, as if the motion could steady the churning.

Alan's eyes followed her movements, and he smiled, glad that she was suffering too. Taking an equally deep gulp of air, he rolled over, his eyes closed, his hands laced together, pillowing his head. He lay like this for a long time before he answered. When he did, his voice was again velvet smooth, no hint of passion.

"It's like this, Megan. I figure that it's time for the farmer to take a wife, and I figure that it's time the farmer's son had a mother. Rosa's been good to us, but Matt needs a mother. Furthermore," he continued, turning his head, his eyes locking with hers, "it's about time Rosa thought about her own life, and she and George have something going. Most important, Megan, I need a wife, and I want you."

Megan crossed her legs in front of herself. "I don't know," she said, refusing to meet his candid gaze. Not a word about love, she thought, but how could there be? Neither one was in love with the other. At least he was honest with her. That was more than she could say for Shane. She shook her head. Was liking someone enough for a good marriage?

"I hadn't thought about marriage," she said defensively. "Really, I hadn't."

His voice went soft and dangerously persuasive. "Neither had I until I met you, Megan." Her eyes widened, and her brows arched in disbelief. "The minute I saw you, Megan, I wanted you, not just physically," he explained. "I wanted you by my side for all time."

"We don't love each other," Megan contended, picking the first argument she could think of.

"Is my loving you so important?" he asked, his eyes searching her face, diligently looking for the truth.

She shrugged. His words were weakening her defenses, and she found herself wanting to say yes, to agree to marry him. Yet she had a nagging doubt. She needed to know more about his first marriage.

"What about Linda?"

He nodded; he understood. "About eight years ago, when I was with Glynn's, I met a model by the name of Linda Mendoza. We fell in love and were married. The first year was wonderful." Then he added grimly, "So I thought. Then I learned that Linda had married me because I was a stepping-stone to greater things." His eyes never left her face, and they compelled her total allegiance. "I was a young executive, moving with the right crowd. That's what Linda loved and wanted, not me.

When someone more useful came along, she left me." The sound of his voice hushed, but the anguish and bitterness hung like a heavy vapor over them. "I thought I would die, but I didn't." Megan waited patiently, hurting for him, knowing he would eventually tell her what she wanted to hear. "We were separated for a year before she called, wanting us to make up. This time, however, she insisted that we live in the country, and I agreed. I bought the farm, and we moved out here. Fool I was," he expostulated vehemently. "When she got tired of being the country belle, she informed me that she still didn't love me, never had. She'd come back only because she thought she was pregnant, and she wanted me to father her baby."

"Matt's not your child?" Megan questioned in surprise.

"Oh, yes," he corrected her, "Matt's my child. All mine!" Megan heard the possessive note in his voice. "Thinking she was pregnant, Linda didn't take any precautions and neither did I; consequently, she did conceive. She hated every minute of it, and she despised both me and the child she carried. Not long after Matt was born, she abandoned both of us." An infinitesimal pause. "She died four years later." The statement was curt and brittle. "She was coming home."

"You loved her," Megan whispered, the words hardly audible above the knot in her throat.

"I loved her," he agreed, then added, "but I hated her too."

Before Megan was aware of what had happened, his hands grasped her by the shoulders, easing her to the ground beside him. Once again they were ensconced in the bed of green grass, Megan flat on her back, Alan leaning over her. Explanations were over; he was through talking.

"That's the past, Megan. It's over and done with. Now I'm living for the future, for you and me. I want a wife, a home, and a mother for my child . . . for my children." Softly he coaxed, "Marry me."

Megan stared at him, temporarily forgetting Linda, captured by the longing she read in his face. She studied the green eyes, which were closely peering into hers. She read their message, and she wanted to respond. Yet she wasn't sure, but then Alan wasn't asking for or proclaiming love. Nor was he promising her love. He was promising her a good, happy marriage. He was promising her security.

"Give me a chance to make you happy, Megan, to make myself happy."

Megan smiled. The man and his argument were persuasive. Lying in the shade of the gnarled oak tree, looking into his beautiful eyes, she was tempted to say yes, but still she held back.

"I'm not convinced that marriage would make either of us happy," she returned truthfully. "What if we married, and Matt didn't like me? What if I couldn't make him a good mother? And I've got to think about becoming the mother to a five-year-old child. That's an awesome responsibility." She moved from the shelter of his arms, sitting up, drawing her knees to her chest, wrapping her arms around her legs and resting her chin on her knees. "I need to think about it."

The air cracked with tension as the silence lengthened between them. Finally Alan spoke. "I guess you do need time to think. I hadn't thought about your end of it. I was selfishly thinking of my own needs and desires." He sprinted up, lowering a hand to help her. "Let's get going. I've got to meet Fitzpatrick."

He jerked her up, and she fell across the hard wall of his chest, his arms closing around her. "Furthermore, I don't dare stay in this oasis with you, Megan, because I want more than a few hugs and kisses. I want to love you, and if we stayed here much longer, I'd do just that." He didn't kiss her again; he just held her closely, resting his cheek against the top of her head. "When are you leaving?"

"Tomorrow," she whispered, her head brushing the muscle-thickness of his shoulder.

She felt his body tense. "Tomorrow?"

"I've got to go," she mumbled sadly. "I've got to get things ready for work on Monday."

"I'll see you tonight?" His breath fanned the silken strands of her hair.

"Yes," she promised, knowing she shouldn't agree to see him again, remembering his words, *It's inevitable.* But at the same time that's why she had to see him.

## CHAPTER FIVE

"What do you mean," Megan demanded, following Alan to the back of the car, "you're coming to Dallas with me?"

"Just that," he said, grunting as he lifted the lid and threw his two valises into the trunk. "I've got to tend to some business, so I figured I might as well drive in with you."

"Just coincidental?" Megan questioned suspiciously, albeit happily.

"Not really," he returned, locking the trunk, walking to the driver's side. "But I decided to tend to it sooner than I would have otherwise." He grasped the handle and opened the door.

Megan grinned. "I don't mind your riding with me—" She stopped talking and chuckled when she saw him slide under the steering wheel. Opening her door, she said, "I don't mind your driving my car for me, but—"

"But what?" Alan asked, grinning devilishly, turning the key and revving the engine. "Are you going to lay down some rules before we even begin our day?" Throwing his arm on the back of the seat, he turned, backing the car out of the drive. "Bismarck," he addressed the dog in an overly dramatic tone, "how can you abide a mistress who's so cantankerous?" Bismarck yawned unconcernedly, and Megan laughed.

"You're not going to win the affection of my dog, so quit trying."

"Ladybug," he said, a smile on his face but seriousness in his eyes and in his tone, "I couldn't care less about winning the affection of your dog. I'm interested in winning your affection."

"Alan," Megan pleaded, "please don't. We went over this again and again last night."

"I still want to marry you," he said, totally unrepentant.

"I can't, I told you. I've got to go back and straighten things out."

"If you married me, you wouldn't have to go back," he pointed out, turning off the dirt road onto the paved road.

"At this point that would be more a cop-out than a solution," she explained. "And even though it does sound inviting, it's not a very good reason for marriage." She shook her head. "Besides, marrying like this wouldn't be fair."

"For whom?" he demanded.

"For either of us."

"If I could be happy, why couldn't you?"

Megan grinned at him, squirming into a comfortable position. "I don't mind your driving me back to Dallas, Farmer McDonald, but we're not going to spend the next few hours that we're shut up in this small car rehashing what we've already hashed. You've got two alternatives: either shut up or drive by yourself."

"Okay, Megan," Alan conceded with good grace, sighing regretfully, his lips twitching into that partial smile. "Have it all your way. Our trip to Dallas will be full of nonsensical prattle. I promise that I won't intrude into your private affairs anymore."

Megan reclipped the bright blue barrette that kept her

hair from her forehead and smiled. Then her hands dropped to the blue and white knit collar of her T-shirt. Her gray eyes danced despite her effort to appear stern. When Alan grinned like that, she couldn't help but melt.

And, at the same time that she was chiding him, she was glad he was with her and that he was persisting. He filled her with excitement and exuberance, infusing vitality and life into her. She lifted her hand, gently running her fingers down the softness of her cheeks. As she did so her eyes caught and held his, her fingers staying their movement.

A caress couldn't have been more potent if it had been physical. The green eyes, warm foliage, sparkling spring green, promised a delightful romp, a pleasurable excursion. They flitted across the fullness of her pink lips, tenderly insinuating, titillating her senses, causing her heart to flutter erratically.

"But, Meggie, if just once . . ." he promised. "Just once, you open that door, I'll rush in, bombard you, and you'll —"

"And I'll," Megan interrupted with a mischievous gurgle, "just suffer the consequences." How smug she was! Grinning! Her eyes dancing, almost a blue-gray!

Alan shook his head, chuckling soundlessly. "Not quite, Miss Jonas. You'll enjoy the consequences. I'll make sure of that." His eyes twinkled as they rested momentarily on her. "You'll enjoy them very much."

Megan's lips curved beautifully, the smile flowing from her eyes, which were now glinting an evocative smoky gray. The way she felt at the moment, she thought, she agreed with him. The consequences would be all too pleasurable. Just the thought of Alan's making love to her sent a current of electricity running up and down her spine.

"Do you understand?" Alan asked when she didn't offer another comeback.

Her head dipped slightly, and she replied with a muffled giggle, "I understand, O Wise One."

"And do you agree?" he asked, his words breezy with laughter.

"We'll see," she evaded.

"Oh, no," he disagreed heatedly. "We'll not see. We'll set the ground rules up ahead of time." His face swiveled to hers. "That way there can be no misunderstanding."

Megan chuckled. "You're a hard taskmaster."

"Not half as hard as I should have been," he returned. "I've been quite remiss in my duties." Promise gleamed from the depth of his green eyes. "I should have pushed a little harder last night." He chuckled at her sharp intake of breath. "But perhaps I've been given a reprieve. Maybe I've got more time to convince you of my charm and worthiness."

"You've convinced me of both facts," Megan retaliated quickly, "but you haven't convinced me that marriage should be based on anything less than love."

"For someone who doesn't want love, Megan, you're certainly hung up on the idea."

"Not really," she retorted with an airy superiority, "but that does prove my point. Since I don't want love and since I'm not in love, I see no sound basis for a marriage between us. Whether I want love or not doesn't enter into the picture. I'm still prudish or old-fashioned enough to want a marriage of love, not convenience."

"Would your answer have been different," he asked, "if I had told you that I loved you?"

"No, it wouldn't have made any difference," she replied honestly. "I'm not ready for marriage—to you or to anyone." Then she added, "At least not until I see Shane again."

"Why then?" Megan heard the urgency in the question. "You're not thinking about Herrington in romantic terms, are you?"

"No," she sighed, "I just want to wipe the slate clean. I want to be sure that he is fully out of my life."

Unaware of the full effect her words were having on Alan, she was unprepared for his sudden swerve to the shoulder of the highway. Quickly he turned off the ignition and slid across the narrow seat, grasping her shoulders firmly in both hands.

"Herrington is out of your life," he declared in a husky undertone, "and I'm in your life. I'm in your life to stay." The green eyes penetrated her with their dark intensity. "I want a wife, Megan. I want you."

"I don't want to make a commitment right now," she breathed, her voice sinking to a husked whisper, her body responding to his. "Would you settle for an affair?"

"No more affairs," he said with a gentle shake of his head. "They're a dime a dozen, and I just ran out of dimes."

His fingers lightened their touch, gently stroking the feverous flesh underneath the soft knit material of her shirt. Hot tongues of fire lapped through her body, quickly melting any icy resistance, stoking the embers of desire. Her eyes were mesmerized by his, and she was trancelike, leaning closer and closer.

"I want to marry you." His voice was soft, caressive, in its quietness. His lips brushed against hers, his breath fanning against her cheeks. "No one else, Megan. Just you."

She turned her face, seeking his lips, needing them, wanting them. She welcomed the sensuous assault, her eyes closing to the burning desire she saw flaring in Alan's eyes. Her hands, master of their own destiny, glided up his chest, resting against the hard planes, her fingers kneading the pulsating flesh. Then she moaned softly, her lips parting, one hand flying to the back of his neck to pull his lips closer to hers.

With a snarl of approval his hand cupped the back of

113

her head, his fingers splaying in the springy masses of her hair, his lips grinding into the softness of hers. His tongue, waiting for no further invitation, burrowed into the musky sweetness of her mouth, and his hands, at the same time, assaulted her elsewhere, gaining an easy victory.

When his fingers gently curved around her breast, she gasped for pleasure, and her hand covered his as she writhed beneath the bombardment of delightful ecstatic chaos. Not aware of its happening, she slipped farther and farther down in the seat, losing herself in the heat of desire, abandoning herself to the moment, knowing only that she wanted to be pleased and to please.

Now she was aware of his hand at the waistband of her knickers. The work-hardened fingertips brushed over the burning flesh, her trembling spurring him on. The language of his body told her of his needs more graphically, more eloquently than any words she had heard in a long time. She forgot they were stopped on the shoulder of the road; she forgot everything but his touch.

Her only thought was to take as much from him as she could. She had never tasted the food of desire before, and she was foundering herself. She enjoyed the spinning, the floating sensation, the losing and not caring, the pushing aside of hurtfulness for all time. His fingers were playing with the elastic of her panties when she heard Bismarck growl in the back seat, and she was suddenly jarred from their little world.

"Hey, fellow!" a deep and gruff voice bellowed above the pounding on the window. "Having trouble?"

Startled to the present, Megan opened her eyes and fought to sit up. Her wide gray eyes stared into the dark sunglasses of the state patrolman who was peering intently into the driver's window. In no hurry, Alan straightened, running his hands through his rusty waves.

"I said, are you having any trouble?" the patrolman repeated, his lips curling into a warm smile.

"Wasn't until you showed up," Alan returned dryly, turning in the seat, rolling down the window at the same time. He darted Megan a quick glance and smiled when he saw the rich redness that stained her cheeks. "Thought I was getting along pretty good."

The officer chuckled softly. "When we saw the car stopped"—with a jerk of his thumb he indicated the other patrolman who still sat in the car—"we figured you were having some trouble."

Alan shook his head. "If this is trouble, officer, I certainly love handling it." Alan could hear Megan's sharp hiss of outrage over the policeman's laughter. "I was just convincing her of my honest intentions," Alan explained.

The officer stepped back, adjusted the glasses on his nose, and eased the wide-brimmed hat back on his forehead. Only his grin kept his words from being cold and austere.

"I'm sure her parents would be happy to know your intentions are honorable," he agreed, "but—" he rolled his eyes and glanced around "—this is hardly the time or the place. If nothing is wrong with the car, how about moving it on out?"

Alan switched on the ignition, unperturbed by the officer's friendly advice and subtle teasing. "I was just fixing to do that."

"By the way," the patrolman added, "in case you're interested, there's a mighty fine motel in the next town."

"How embarrassing!" Megan fumed, her face still glowing crimson. "What do you think he thought?"

Alan chuckled, grabbing her waist, pulling her closer to him before he pulled onto the highway again. "I know what he thought," Alan confessed. "I bet he wished I was sitting in the patrol car with that bulldog face and he was sitting in this car with you."

Megan laughed, squirming to see the other patrolman.

"Well," she admitted, "I can understand why. That's a dour-faced one if I've ever seen one."

Alan's fingers laced through hers, and he rubbed his jaw with the back side of her hand. "Shall we take the patrolman up on the motel?" Alan persisted, his voice velvet soft and sensuous.

"I don't *think* so," Megan whispered, her luminous gray eyes dissolving into his.

"Sure?" he asked quietly, and as Megan nodded her head, she knew that he was hoping for more. Yet he never allowed his disappointment to show.

She laid her head on his shoulder, letting her mind wander, sifting through her thoughts and memories at random, remembering all the good times she and Alan had shared during the past week. And as Alan began to talk, the little town of Los Nogalitos slid miles and miles behind them. The golden brightness of the spring morning turned into the glaring sunburst of afternoon and fused into the flowing grayness of early evening.

Alan jarred Megan from her light sleep by shaking his shoulder. "We're here."

She sat up, raked her fingers through her hair, and stared about her for a minute, getting her bearings. "What time is it?"

He flicked his wrist. "Nine." She nodded but didn't say anything. "How does it feel to be back home?"

She shrugged. "Okay, I guess." Then she confessed. "But I like Los Nogalitos better."

"Maybe this isn't your home," he concluded with a happy softness. "Maybe you're not a city girl."

She smiled, snugging up to him, squeezing as much comfort from him as she could. "Could be!" She stared out the window for a while. "Where are you staying?"

Easily weaving from one expressway to another, Alan told her the name of the hotel. "Is that on your way or not?"

116

"Not really," she confessed, giving him the directions to her apartment. "I don't mind dropping you off by your hotel, however." But even as she said the words, she knew she was lying. She didn't want to leave him, and a feeling of sadness descended over her. The glare of the city lights mocked her; they jeered her loneliness.

Alan sensed her reluctance to let him go, and he capitalized on it. "How about our eating dinner first?"

Megan shook her head. "Love to, but I need to let Bismarck run awhile."

"Do you have anything in the apartment to fix?"

"We'll make do," she responded laconically with a smile.

"I'll bet your cupboard is as bare as Joel's was," he retorted. "And you need something substantial to eat."

"What about Bismarck?" she questioned, wanting his company as much as he wanted hers.

Alan laughed. "I wish you cared as much for me as you do that dog. We'll go by your apartment and drop Bismarck off. Then I'll take you for a quick meal. How about that?"

Megan nodded, her smile never fading. "Fine as long as I don't have to dress up. I'm too tired." Then she proceeded to give him the directions to her house again.

While she talked, Alan gave her the once-over. "You look fine to me," he commented truthfully, taking in the knit shirt and white knickers.

Megan giggled. "I'm sure I do," she responded dramatically. "My knickers are all wrinkled from riding, and my hair needs combing."

"Fishing for a compliment?" Alan wheedled.

"Not really," she returned with spirit. "I just don't want to get out looking like this."

"Tell you what," Alan suggested. "While we're at your place, you can shower and change clothes, and we'll stop by the hotel and I'll do the same."

"Why not," Megan quipped. This might be the last time she saw Farmer McDonald. Might as well make the most of it! Her smile deepened and lingered warmly in her eyes.

It wasn't long afterward that they were parked under the carport at her apartment. Megan fastened Bismarck's leash to his collar and took him for a walk while Alan unloaded the car, carrying her suitcases into the house. By the time she joined him he was standing in the living room, replacing the telephone on the cradle.

"I just called the hotel," he informed her, looking around, taking in the apartment. "If it's okay with you, we'll have dinner in my room."

Megan threw him an uneasy glance as she kneeled to unfasten Bismarck's leash.

Seeing her grimace of displeasure and doubt, Alan quickly pointed out, "That way you won't have to dress, and we can enjoy a good meal."

"I don't think so," Megan began with an unequivocal shake of her head, standing up at the same time.

He smiled, dropping his hands until they casually rested on his hips. "It's okay, Meggie. I've got a full suite," his eyes mocked her, "and I promise not to make a move without your approval."

She eyed him skeptically. That was the least of her fears. Her inability to handle her emotions was her greatest fear.

"I mean it," he said solemnly, raising his right hand. "Scout's honor." Although his eyes danced with undisguised merriment, his lips didn't so much as twitch.

Megan read the challenge; she read the message. He knew her fear also, but he was gambling. He was daring her to come. And, she thought with an arrogant toss of her head, she'd prove to him that she was stronger than he. She wouldn't give in to his demands. Tentatively she nodded her head, licking her bottom lip. The words from yesterday kept ringing out with a clarion peal: *It's inevitable, Megan.*

She walked to the kitchen, hanging Bismarck's leash on the key ring on the wall. Then she lifted his dish, filling it with fresh water and food.

"Well?" Alan asked from the door, afraid she was going to refuse. He had learned during the past week that Megan Jonas could be a very stubborn woman, a woman who was determined to have her own way, a person not easily pushed into making a decision. So, he wisely decided, he wouldn't push her. He'd give her plenty of room. He kept his voice clearly impersonal. "Are you or not? I need to know so I can cancel the dinner if you're not."

"Yes," she replied matter-of-factly, brushing her hands down the side of her pants. "I'm going. Let me take care of Bismarck and shower." She set the dog's dish on the placemat on the floor. "I'll be ready in a minute."

Alan drew a silent breath of relief, following her through the apartment into the bedroom, watching as she began to jerk open drawers. "Am I invited to bathe with you?"

Lifting her underwear out of the drawer, Megan said, "Not tonight." She strove for a nonchalance she was far from feeling. She walked to the closet and took out her fresh outfit, holding it up for Alan to see.

"You can't be missed in that," he said, liking the bright sunshine colors that splashed together in large squares.

Megan grinned. "I thought so too." She fished through her jewelry box, coming out with three large plastic bracelets, one red, one blue, and one yellow.

Alan watched her with a fond intentness. "How about in the morning?"

Laying the bracelets on the dresser, she turned, looking at him blankly. "In the morning?"

"What about my bathing with you in the morning?"

She moved into the bathroom, slamming the door after herself. He heard the unmistakable click of the lock.

"We'll let the morning take care of itself." Then he heard the spray of the shower.

Alan chuckled, moving around the room slowly, carefully, scrutinizing everything, learning as much about Megan as he could. "Don't take too long," he called. "I've already ordered dinner."

"I won't," she sang out above the gurgling water.

And she didn't. About fifteen minutes later she stepped into the living room. "How do I look?" She pirouetted in front of him, pulling the bracelets over her hand.

The green eyes swept up and down her slim figure several times appreciatively. "Just beautiful," he whistled softly. "No one can accuse you of being dull."

Her skin gleamed a copper tone and was complemented by the spaghetti straps that tied over her shoulders. The blousy cover-up shimmered, hanging down to her waist, and the soft voile culottes gently draped over her hips, enhancing the beauty of her legs. A pair of light colored sandals laced up around her ankles.

"Altogether pretty," he proclaimed, his eyes raking over her again. "I'll be delighted to escort you through the lobby to my suite, Miss Jonas."

She picked up her purse and walked over to him, hooking her arm in his. "And I'll be delighted to accompany you, Farmer McDonald." The excitement that bubbled through her veins also shined in her eyes. "Shall we go?"

Alan's eyes sparkled into hers. "We shall, Miss Jonas."

Exhilarated and effervescent, Megan accompanied Alan to the car, her happiness not diminishing a whit as they continued their verbal sparring in the car. And when they walked through the lobby, Megan's brilliant smile and glowing radiance attracted the glances of many passersby, filling Alan with pride.

"Why a suite?" she asked as Alan unlocked the doors to his rooms.

"It's what I want," he replied succinctly. "Besides, it's

the only way the company can persuade me to join in these conferences."

"Are they that bad?" she asked laughingly.

"Have been," he returned, striding into the bedroom, throwing his suitcase on a stool. As quickly, he began to strip. "Make yourself at home," he enjoined briskly, walking into the bathroom. "I'm going to take a shower." She heard the shower spray. "You wouldn't consider taking another one, would you?" he called out.

Megan laughed, but the color seeped into her face as she thought about the intimacy of a shower with Alan. "Not tonight."

Megan heard his quiet laughter as he shut the bathroom door. Then the hushed quietness of the room began to obliterate her confidence. She felt confined and restricted; she felt vulnerable and gauche. Apprehension caused cold sweat to pop out in the palms of her hands as the minutes slowly ticked by. She almost jumped when she heard him speak directly behind her.

"Has room service brought the wine yet?" Although fully dressed, he vigorously rubbed his damp hair with a towel.

His presence filled the room, devastating Megan with his masculine aura. His designer jeans were immaculate, new, and expensive. His knit shirt, green and white, accentuated his broad shoulders and enhanced the color of his eyes.

Not needing the wine, Megan drank in his virility, shaking her head and mumbling "No."

A phone call, she thoughtly numbly, not moving from her spot, a soft, but firm, command, and a sharp rap at the door soon afterward. The caddy rolled in, Alan poured the wine—one glass, two, she forgot how many—a succulent feast followed. Freely drinking and pleasurably eating the meal, Megan allowed herself to relax, to be enveloped by the warmth and charm of Alan McDonald. She allowed

121

herself to be completely disarmed. Her hunger appeased, she untied her shoes, kicked them off, and burrowed into the corner of the sofa, listening to his soft voice, and sipped another glass of wine.

Alan lounged in the large, overstuffed chair, his legs stretched out in front of him, his stockinged feet crossed at the ankles. With indolent grace he dangled the wine-glass loosely in his hand which drooped over the end of the chair arm.

His eyes weren't closed, but they were hooded by his thick russet lashes, and they were shaded by the muted glow from the lamp. He stared at the woman across the room from him. He felt a hunger stirring in his loins that demanded satisfaction, a hunger that hadn't been satiated since he'd met Megan. To the contrary, every meeting with her had increased the yearning.

He lifted the glass to his lips, savouring the dryness of the wine. Over the rim his emerald eyes focused on Megan, but she was—or did she just appear to be—impervious to his longings and achings. Her gray eyes, relaxed and somnolent, moved impersonally over the hotel room, which she didn't like or dislike; she felt nothing about it. She was, however, aware suddenly of Alan's steady gaze.

Slowly her eyes pivoted to his, fusing with the gentle green. As slowly, as cautiously, she smiled, the tip of her tongue running over her lips. Her heart beat faster as she gazed into those amorous eyes, blatantly flashing his wants and demands. It wasn't hard for her to guess his thoughts, to sense his wants. Dropping her gaze, she wondered if he could see the same wanting in her.

The thick rust lashes lifted; the green eyes, bright with a question, silently observed the dove softness of hers just before she lowered her lids. And she couldn't, wouldn't, meet his point-blank assault again. Nervously she lifted the glass to her lips, drinking but not tasting the wine.

With irritable movements her fingers curled and uncurled around the stem of the glass.

*Dear Lord,* she summoned silently, *I've got to get out of here.* Without her being aware of it, the gray eyes flitted around the room as if she were seeking a route of escape. The walls were closing in on her. All she could see was Alan; all she could think was Alan; she could smell him, hear him. Most of all, she wanted to taste him. Her mouth, her tongue, her hands, all clamored for the heady delights that he had promised her.

Making the decision, pushing forward, she grabbed her shoes, hastily slipping her feet into them. "I've—I've got to go." She didn't dare look into those mockery-filled eyes.

"Really?" he questioned slowly, unbelievingly, some-how covering the distance that separated them, somehow on the sofa beside her, throwing the shoes on the floor. "Why the hurry?"

His hands closed over her fingers, and he lifted them, kissing the tip of each finger. His lips feathered lightly over each, brushing and teasing. Megan tried to twist away from him, but he edged closer, pressing her into the cushiony softness of the sofa.

"How about another glass of wine?" he suggested, his eyes hotly seductive, golden glints spiraling from the dark green centers.

Megan breathed deeply, her head saying no, her mouth saying yes. She was already light-headed from the wine and she didn't need any more, but she wanted to get him away from her. This would divert his attention. It would get her out of his arms.

"I think I will," she croaked, her throat dry.

His nearness caused her to react impulsively rather than reasonably, she thought irritably as he smiled condescend-ingly at her, inching away. Ordinarily she wouldn't have drunk so freely, but tonight she wasn't thinking. The irony of it all, she thought, disgusted with herself, was she didn't want to think. She wanted to react, to respond to whatever Alan asked.

Still smiling, he stood and walked to the caddy that rested in the center of the room. He lifted the bottle from the ice in which it was wrapped and poured both of them a glass. As if mesmerized, Megan watched him move in her direction, lifting one of the glasses to his lips, sipping the sparkling beverage. He turned the glass around, handed it to her, and watched to see if she would place her lips over the imprint of his.

"Don't go home." The words were an intimate plea. "Stay with me."

Hypnotized by his movements, by his soft words, Megan didn't have the will to break eye contact. Her hands reached out to take the glass, but she was so intent on looking at him that her fingers didn't quite reach the stem. The glass slipped from her fingers, spilling the wine on the carpet.

"I'm sorry," she blurted out, galvanized into action, springing to her feet.

"Don't worry about it," Alan said dismissively, handing her the other glass. "What's a glass of wine, more or less, between friends?"

Nervously Megan gulped the wine, pacing around the room that was growing smaller and smaller each minute. She knew she had to leave. She knew it! But, she thought resignedly, she didn't want to leave. She wanted to stay here with him; she wanted to be comforted; she wanted to be loved. Her eyes sought his. She wanted to be loved by Alan McDonald.

He read the answer. "Staying?" The word softly drifted to her.

Fidgeting, she walked to the terrace doors, stood in the late evening breeze, the tendrils of hair fanning around her face. She shouldn't have come. She had known that from the beginning. Yet she had dared him. She had dared herself! Now she regretted her decision. She didn't have the will to refuse her body's raging needs and desires. She blinked her eyes and shook her head, hoping to dispel the hazy lethargy and acceptance that descended on her.

"No." The word was light and breezy, and it lacked conviction. How could it? She was lying; she wanted to stay. She was almost drunk, too, she thought, looking at the empty glass in her hand. How many had she had?

Alan continued to watch her, his eyes soft and gentle, an enigmatic smile playing around the corners of his mouth. He knew she was lying, and he knew she wasn't leaving. His eyes never left her, following each agitated movement. She turned, flinging her head over her shoulder, her back to him, glancing furtively at him. She raised her hand and brushed the back of it across her forehead and eyes.

He sensed her fear, her anxieties, and he moved. She didn't hear him, but she felt him. No, she didn't really feel him; rather she sensed his presence, his strength, his warmness, his vitality. She smelled the aftershave lotion that wafted in the soft breeze, the musky odor of his bath soap, the tangy wine on his breath. She felt the hardness of his chest behind her shoulders, the flat plane of his stomach running along her spine, the narrow swell of his hips against the curving softness of her buttocks.

She felt his hands on her shoulders, turning her around, his fingers taking the wineglass from her unresisting hands. She thought she heard a thud as it hit the carpet, but she couldn't be sure. She didn't care. Her eyes closed, and she waited for his lips.

Was she breathing? She couldn't be sure. She was inhaling quickly, but her chest hurt. His hands were on her everywhere, anywhere, all at once. Her hands chased his, twisting, squirming, unsuccessfully evading, but never escaping the erotic encroachment.

"No, Alan." Did she speak? Did that wobbling voice belong to her?

"Yes," he whispered urgently, his hands cupping her chin and her neck, his thumbs stroking the sensitive fullness of her red lips. "You want this to happen as much as I do, Megan. Both of us need it. Besides," he added in the husky undertone, "you knew it was going to happen sooner or later."

Valiantly she struggled to open her eyes, to think. She had to get away from him. She had to leave, didn't she? The words reverberated, bouncing around inside her head. They were just that—words, nothing more. Words with no meaning. Words with no command. Words with no action. Still she fought to give them meaning, summoning her wayward mind, trying to inject command in them. Just as perversely and persistently, Alan fought to obstruct the meaning for her, his commands countering any order she issued.

"Later," she mumbled incoherently. "Later, please. I've got to go now."

Speaking softly against her ear, Alan said, "No, not later, and you aren't going to leave. You're staying with me."

"Yes," she breathed, accepting the inevitable, succumbing to the argument and the tidal wave of desire, her resolve crumbling into submission. "Just for the night?"

If it were just for the night, she wouldn't have the strength left to fight it, she knew, but she wanted him to admit more. She wanted to hear the words once again. She wanted to be reassured.

His lips in tender assault, lovingly gentle, pressed against hers, lifting enough that he could answer. "No, not just for tonight. I want you for the rest of my life."

His fingers stroked her shoulders, and she felt her blouson fall, leaving her breasts bare, firmly uptilted, the nipples proudly peaking. Her eyes opened wide, and she stared wildly into his face. His eyes, however, never noted her shock because he was feasting on the sight of her. His face lowered, and his lips nibbled and bit along the satiny swell until he reached the rosy crest. His mouth closed over it; reverently his tongue swirled slowly around the inflamed peak, his mouth sucking with infinite tenderness.

Megan groaned softly, her stomach churning with an insatiable hunger, moving instinctively against his hard frame, her hands holding the back of his head, pressing him closer, drawing him closer, defying him to leave her. Frantically she held on, afraid she'd fall if she didn't. Her legs felt like jelly, and evocative splinters pricked her all over. She twisted her shoulders, swaying her breasts, softly sighing, vividly aware of the growing hunger, the aching hunger inside her.

When Alan lifted his head, gathered her into his arms, and carried her to the bedroom, she offered no argument. She didn't know what the future held for them, but she knew that she wanted him, wanted the pleasure he promised, wanted the fulfillment he promised. She couldn't imagine in her wildest ruminations that she would be the source of pleasure and fulfillment for him.

She lay on the bed and through misty eyes, watched him quickly shed his clothes. The socks were discarded first, the shirt tossed over them, the jeans landing in a heap with them. In the dim light that streamed in from the living room, she saw him standing there beside the bed, naked and powerful.

He sat down on the bed beside her, and she, as if hypnotized, lifted her shoulders, easing the elasticized waist of her culottes over her hips, wriggling out of them. Again she watched with fascination as he caught them, hurling them into a far corner of the room.

His fingers hooked at the elastic band of her bikini panties, and his eyes, now a deep hunter green, shaded, blazed brightly with passion. He lowered himself on the bed at the same time that his lips began to whisper down her neck, over her breasts, the flatness of her stomach. A twist, a yank, a few more undefined movements and she lay beside him naked, her body glowing in the muted light.

His lips traced the outline of her collarbone, his hands exploring her body leisurely, delighting her with their wondrous discoveries, thrilling her with fevered search, moist and warm. His pleasure heightened with her inarticulate moans and cries, her heady breathing, her whimpers of joy.

His fingers traced paths of fire up her inner thighs, treading lightly over her intimately, causing her body to convulse with raw desire. Her blood coursed through her veins, pounded through her head, each pulse station beating, beating, beating! She couldn't have resisted his touch. She wouldn't have! It was divine! It was exquisite torment!

Never had she ridden this high on sensuous pleasure before, moving with him, for him, against him, her body perfectly in tune with his every command and desire. Never had she known what perfect communion between man and woman was. She had never shared this with Shane. She had never dreamed it was possible to feel this way.

Her hands grasped the hair at the nape of his neck, and she guided his face up to hers. Her hot fevered lips captured his, and she pulled his warm moist body over hers, his hair-matted chest touching her throbbing peaks, the flat stomach rubbing against her soft one, the hardness of his lower body gently seeking entrance to the musky sweetness of her body.

His knee wedged itself between her thighs, carefully spreading her legs apart, as carefully he lowered himself into position. She was ready; he knew. She wanted him; she needed him as much as he wanted and needed her.

*Careful,* he thought. He had to be careful with her. *I must tread softly,* he admonished himself. Make it good!

Make it unforgettable! Wipe out Shane's memory once and for all! He would. He could give her greater pleasure than Shane had. He would make her love him. He would make her marry him. *And,* he thought, *I'll love her. God,* he confessed, *I love her now.*

They would be good for each other, he resolved, his hand stroking her cheek with reverential tenderness.

"Oh, Meggie," he sighed, easing his body lower, farther, more intimately, "you're so sweet, so very sweet." His lips closed on hers, parting them wider, wider, his tongue probing, filling her mouth, the tip exploring, searching, titillating.

She stiffened, tensed momentarily, her face twisting from his, a small gasp of fear on her lips. She felt his hardness. The pain . . . The shock . . . Then she relaxed, two tears falling down the side of her face.

Surprise first, then wondrous astonishment registered on Alan's face. His hands cupped her firm buttocks, and he held her close, his movements stopping. With practiced expertise, with determined skill, but mostly with tenderness and love, he stroked and loved her, whispering words of love, of endearment, of encouragement in her ears, his lips finally catching hers again, his tongue slipping into the moistness of her mouth as he moved into the warm haven of her intimacy, stroking, rekindling the flame of desire.

Her lips began to tug gently, sipping the sweetness, her tongue returning the strokes, fighting for entrance into the depth of his mouth. Instinctively her body began to respond, her hands of their own volition, with no guidance from him, began to caress, to stroke, to give joy. Her hips swayed with his motion, heightening his anticipation. Their fevered moans of pleasure were thick and inaudible.

Together they ran through the grassland of pleasurable delight, climbing the hill together, breathlessly falling down on the top, gasping for air. They smiled into each

129

other's face, their eyes burning with feverous passion, glazed with longing and wanting. Then they stared upward at the golden brightness of the sun, watching it turn from soft gold to orange to bright red, exploding into little pieces that drifted and floated, landing here and there.

They lay in the sublime peace of a verdant green hillside, lingering in the afterglow, hardly moving, barely breathing, not daring to break the spell that bound them together. They reveled in their rapturous moment of togetherness, that moment that no one, nothing, could take from them.

Her shudders ceased, her trembling quieted, and she lay in the security of his arms, her face hidden in the mat of dark red hair that covered his chest. She breathed deeply, filling her lungs with the smell of him, her heartbeat slowly returning to normal.

"I knew you were innocent," he said, "but I didn't know . . . how innocent." Reflectively he said, "I figured you'd gone further with Shane."

"I hadn't," she murmured.

"Why didn't you tell me?"

"Why should I?" she returned quietly. "It wouldn't have mattered, would it?" She added the question as an afterthought, her face pulling away from the warmth of his body, her eyes peering into his.

"No," he murmured lovingly. "It wouldn't have made any difference. I just thought you may have wanted to wait until we were married."

Assured, contented once again, she snuggled down, shaking her head, drifting to sleep. "No," she mumbled, "this is the way I wanted it."

"You are going to marry me," he insisted.

She didn't answer; she was already asleep. Then he closed his arms around her, his eyelids fluttering down also. Through the long night he cradled her close to him, rousing every so often with the delightful memories of the evening before. Finally, however, he drifted into a deeper sleep, not awakening until he heard the shrill, persistent jangle of the phone.

Disengaging his arms and legs from Megan, he rolled over and picked up the receiver. "Hello," he answered, his voice thick and raspy with sleep.

Megan, rousing with him, turned also, her fingers twining in the soft hairs on his chest, her lips pouting, inviting his nipples to peak.

She heard Alan chuckle. "Sorry I stood you up, love, but I had a more pressing engagement."

Megan stiffened. Whom was he talking to? Alan looked down at her and shook his head, his hand running down the length of her naked body.

He spoke again. "I think she's worth it. I intend to marry her." A pause. "I don't know if I'll introduce her before the wedding or not." Megan could hear the laughter that weaved the words together. "Yes, Mother," he sighed resignedly, "I'm going to introduce her to you and Skipper."

Megan giggled and snugged up to Alan, her curiosity and jealousy satisfied.

"Okay," he said, and Megan could tell that he was going to hang up, "we'll be out for dinner tonight."

As he clamped the receiver down, he turned and grabbed Megan to him, stilling her errant fingers and mouth. His lips captured hers in a long, satisfying kiss.

"Now, Miss Jonas," he announced with a flourish, sweeping the covers aside, "I'm going to teach you all the intricacies of taking a bath with a man."

Megan blushed beautifully, glowing, a woman in love, but she didn't move when he stood and held out his hand.

He chided her gently, "Meggie, you're not embarrassed?"

She shook her head. "No, I'm not embarrassed," she announced. "I'm just wondering if bathing with you can be any more exciting than sleeping with you."

Alan threw back his head and laughed, a deep sonorous rumble that came from deep within. "Come and see, my love. Come and see."

## CHAPTER SIX

Megan's hair was pulled into a beautiful knot on the top of her head, with soft breathy curls wisping around her face. Her gray eyes were wide and luminous with a twinge of apprehension glittering in their depths, but even this didn't diminish their beauty. They sparkled, enhanced by the crisp gray linen of her suit and the mauve softness of her blouse.

Reaching up, she pulled the combs from her hair, carefully placing them on her dressing table, absently looking at herself in the mirror. Her eyes, happily dancing with memories as she thought of the past week, grew dreamy and pensive, and her lips parted to curve upward, a soft sigh whispering through the room.

Without conscious thought she twirled around, sitting in the antique slipper rocker, taking off her high-heeled shoes, dropping them at her feet. First she squirmed out of her pantyhose, letting it fall to the floor beside her shoes. Then she lifted her left hand and gazed lovingly at the wide gold band Alan had given her. She twisted her fingers, letting the huge diamond sparkle in the dim light.

All this time, she gently chided herself, she had thought

Alan was rough and uncivilized, completely lacking in the amenities of urban culture. Foolish woman! During the past week she had learned differently. Perhaps if things hadn't happened as quickly as they had, she would have changed her mind about marrying him. As it was, he gave her no time to think about anything. Although he tenderly and gently swept her into marriage, he did it quickly. Because she was so happy, she didn't care. She let herself be rushed willingly.

First in her series of discoveries was the revelation that Alan was quite wealthy and that his grandfather was the department store magnate, William Harrison Glynn. To say she was surprised would be a vast understatement. She had been shocked; then she had been dubious.

But Alan had hastily dispelled her uncertainties and doubts. He assured her that as long as his mother remained president of the company, he planned to reside in Los Nogalitos, coming into Dallas only when it proved necessary. Of course, he added, the time would come when they would return to Dallas to live permanently. At such time, Rosa and George, who were soon to be married, would manage the dairy farm for him.

Then Megan had met Alan's family, his mother, Alanna McDonald, and his grandfather, nicknamed Skipper. Both welcomed her into the family, Skipper without reservations, Alanna more slowly and cautiously. A soft chuckle escaped Megan's lips as she recalled her introduction to them.

William Harrison Glynn was a gruff old man who spoke rather curtly and brusquely. "Just call me Skipper," he had commanded when he shook hands with her. "That way I still feel like a senior citizen rather than a senile old man." Megan had smiled. "Now I want to know," he had added in a hushed whisper, looking rather conspiratorially at Alan, "what do you think of this grandson of mine?"

Megan had replied mischievously, "I'm not too sure,"

casting Alan a teasing glance of withering disdain, laughing aloud when he grimaced at her.

Skipper had chuckled too. "Me either, my girl. Any good-looking young man who would go bury himself in that deserted part of south Texas, I'm not too sure about myself. However," he pronounced, wagging his index finger in Alan's direction, "he seems to be redeeming himself now. I'm glad he's found something to interest him besides those heifers."

Alan now laughed with gusto. "That proves that you'd better run Glynn's and let me run the dairy business, Skipper. I've just found my heifer." With that Alan winked at Megan.

Although not instantly, Megan had also grown to like Alanna, who was of medium height, slender, and attractive. Though she looked her full fifty-five years, her short hair was naturally black, cut stylishly, gently fringing her face. Like Skipper, she spoke brusquely, but she was sincerely friendly. When she had assured herself that Megan truly loved Alan, she began to drop the cool reserve, and by the end of the evening she and Megan were talking quite comfortably.

Megan learned that Alan's father had died during the Korean War when Alan was a small child, and Alanna with the help of her father had reared Alan alone, never remarrying. Alan, however, had not been one to tie himself down to the business like his grandfather and mother. Both of them blamed his unhappy marriage for this, and both felt that he had buried himself in Los Nogalitos out of grief. Now that he was remarrying, both hoped that he would return to Dallas. But, Megan smiled, that was one decision she would leave to Alan. As for as herself, she would be content to live in Los Nogalitos for the rest of her life.

The opening and closing of the door gently jounced Megan from her ruminations to the present, and she knew that Alan had returned. Her face glowed with happiness, her cheeks were naturally pink, and her lips parted, lifting into a welcome smile. When he walked into the bedroom, dropping his keys and change on the nightstand, her face flushed an even deeper pink. Their eyes caught and held, both savoring the physical essence of the other.

She luxuriated in his presence: his tie, loosely knotted, hanging slackly around his neck, his coat long since discarded, his vest unbuttoned, his shirt sleeves rolled up, exposing his muscular wrists and hands. Not missing a step, he walked to the chair, his eyes filled with worshipful adoration. He held his hands out; she lifted hers.

"Hello, Mrs. McDonald." He pulled her to her feet, not caring that he crushed her blouse, his hands running possessively over her back.

"Hello, Mr. McDonald." Her arms wrapped around his broad shoulders, and her fingers gripped the muscle-corded flesh beneath the expensive shirt.

"You smell good." He breathed in the scent of her body.

His face lifted from the curve of her shoulders, his lips fastening on hers, lightly pressing, breathy and teasing in quality. It wasn't a kiss of passion but one of promise, an enduring caress that would withstand all doubt and uncertainty . . . so Alan thought at the time. It was a loving brand, a possessive touch that said, I belong to you, and you belong to me.

"Do you want me to undress you?"

She heard the soft whisper and felt his hands as they encountered the small round pearl buttons on the front of her blouse.

"No," she whispered in return, stepping from the shelter of his arms. "I want us to undress together." Love had darkened her eyes, and they gleamed a beautiful silvery gray, dancing, alive, suggestive. "I want to look at you, and I want to watch you as you see me undress." She shrugged out of her jacket, looping it over the back of the

136

small rocker, watching as he eased out of his vest, carelessly dropping it in the chair by the bed.

"You're a wampass kitty, Mrs. McDonald," he charged.

Rich color heightened her cheeks, her laughter the music of his soul. "Right you are," she retorted with spirit, her fingers flying to the top buttons of her blouse. "I've had an excellent teacher."

"At least give me a fair chance," he chuckled, glancing at her bare feet, intrigued with her audacity. "You're ahead of me." Sitting on the edge of the bed, he quickly shucked his shoes and socks, leaving them beside her sandals and stockings. When he straightened and stood, they stared at each other a full second before their hands, in unison, began to push each button through the buttonholes.

Never taking their eyes from each other, their fingers worked feverishly, his steadily and slowly moving from the top button to the bottom of his mauve-colored shirt, hers deftly pushing the tiny pearls through the loops. When both the blouse and shirt were unbuttoned, they paused, reading love in each other's eyes, sending love, receiving love.

Never breaking the magic of the moment, she caught the soft fabric, tugged it from her skirt and let it fall apart, not pulling it off her shoulders. Alan did the same with his shirt. Then his hand fell to the clasp of his slacks, and he became the leader.

Megan watched his hands. The waistband parted; the zipper slid down; he kicked out, flexing his strong, powerful legs. Megan's fingers unsnapped the waistband of her skirt, holding it just a second before she let it drop to the floor, stepping out of the circle of gray linen.

They moved together, toward each other, a common command issued from each. Her hands gently feathered beneath the silky material on his shoulders, whisking it off,

137

and his fingers as gently discarded the soft crepe from her shoulders. Each let the material fall to the floor, not giving it another thought.

Megan's eyes misted with passion as she looked at the rugged virility of her husband, her eyes spanning his broad chest, hard and covered with thick springy curls. All she dreamed of, more than she hoped for! Her fingers gently, adoringly, traced designs over his shoulders, down the muscled biceps, then up again. Her mouth, open in wanting and desire, closed over the muscle-distended chest, her tongue swirling, warmly enticing his nipples to bud.

Alan's body shuddered with his longing, and his hand caught in the hair at the nape of her neck, his fingers splaying and closing in the rich thickness. With tender pressure he lifted her face, his lips coming down to capture hers, a small sigh of pleasure escaping just before the moistly hot lips clamped over hers.

Although there was no need, one hand held her face in place, and the other cupped her firmly rounded buttocks, pressing the softness of her body against the throbbing hardness of his. His tongue, finding no resistance, entered into that door of sweet pleasure, stroking and whetting her desire, causing her to writhe against him, causing want to splinter heatedly from her deepest core. He rejoiced in her erotic movements and whispers.

When he finally lifted his lips, she murmured with a husky breathlessness, "You're ahead of me now. I still have my slip—"

Rather than acknowledge this, however, his lips rained soft kisses across her face, her eyes, her cheeks, down the column of her arched throat, down to the fullness of her breasts that peaked over the top of her dusty-pink brassiere, up again to claim her lips in a long and deep kiss, fully satisfying, definitely promising more.

"And your bra," he finally husked, tearing his lips from hers, one hand sliding down from her hair, one gliding from her buttocks to unhook the small band. His fingers caught on the two straps and pulled them off her shoulders, letting the soft nylon fall around her feet. "Now your slip." His fingers caught in the elastic at her waist; he stretched it, eased it over her hips, and let it fall heedlessly to the floor to join the discarded pile of clothes. "Now nothing left but your panties."

His face lowered, his lips fluttering caressively over the smooth round swell, dwelling on the strutted tip, his tongue licking, hot and moistly, sending excruciating waves of pleasure through her body, his hands moving up the flatness of her belly over her midriff, cupping the weight of each breast, gently kneading each.

Megan's fingers curled around his head, her face furrowing into the russet hair, her lips caressingly kissing the luxuriant thickness, inwardly aching for the completeness of their love. Convulsively she trembled her need, the void and emptiness driving shafts of piercing want through her body.

Then his hands feathered across the midriff down the stomach, causing her to quake with desire, causing her to suck her breath in with a gasping sigh, a fiery tingling feathering up her spine. He caught the narrow band of lace, splaying his fingers tormentingly over her skin as he pulled off her bikini.

"At last," he sighed, moving slightly, his tongue teasing her outer ear, chasing thrills down the side of her neck, snugging in the hollow of her shoulders, nipping at the collarbone, the small indention at the base of her neck. He pushed her out of his arms and looked at her—her face, her neck, her shoulders, the pulsating breasts, peaked, uptilted, firmly rounded, thrusting proudly and regally, her flat stomach, her thighs, the dark-tufted triangle.

"Now I see you," he declared with reverential awe, "all of you, and you're beautiful." With a gentle desperation he clutched her to him, lovingly folding her to his chest, clasping her tightly as if he were afraid of losing her. "You belong to me, Megan. You're mine. All mine."

Exulting in the mastery of his touch, excited by his every mention of love, and not angered by his possessiveness, Megan wrapped her arms around him, moving, touching, feeling, thrilling. "I'm yours," she agreed quietly, "just like you're mine." Then she lifted his face from her shoulders, cradling it with the palms of both hands, her thumbs lightly resting under his chin, her fingers stroking his beard-stubbled cheeks. "Now I'm going to finish undressing you," she announced between quick, peppery kisses.

He stood, august as a god, gazing down as she knelt, pulling his briefs over his hips, below his knees, letting them slide to the floor. Her lips, feathering light kisses, followed the path of her fingertips. Falling back on her knees, balancing on the flatness of her two palms, she stared up at him—utterly masculine and majestic.

With a voice tempered with love she said, "I didn't know a man could be so—" She paused, searching for her word. "So beautiful."

Tears shimmered in her eyes, causing them to sparkle like diamonds as she watched Alan kneel beside her. They stretched out together, his gaunt hardness pressing into her softness, making her fully aware of his wants, transmitting the depth of his love to her.

"I never knew love could be so beautiful," he whispered, his mouth moving against the tangle of her hair, his voice ragged and raw, his desires rampant with longing. His hands stroked her length, beginning at her breasts, sweeping down the curve of her waist, her thighs, her ankles, then up again. His hands swept ever wider and wider, and Megan groaned her wants, her needs, her desires.

"Oh, yes," she murmured in a frenzied pitch. The time

didn't matter; the place didn't matter; only the man and the woman mattered.

"Yes," he agreed, his voice a husky parody of its normally vibrant tones.

Her body responded to his every demand, and she learned how to make demands. Both quivered with anticipation. And through the night, long after they moved from the floor to the bed, he tutored her in the fine art of love. Again and again he carried her to the dizzy heights of ecstasy. They declared their love for each other over and over, both joyously laughing at their newly found emotion, the warmness, the tenderness, the oneness. They were drunk on love. It wasn't until sometime during the late hours of morning that they fell into a sated, peaceful sleep.

Megan rolled over, flung one hand over her eyes, shading them from the bright glare of the mid-morning sun. Experimentally she opened first one then the other. She glanced around. Where was she? Her bedroom! She rubbed the back of her hand across her forehead, wincing with pain as a hard object scraped across the tender flesh. She lifted her hand and stared at the unfamiliar ring—a wide yellow gold band with a diamond solitaire in the center. Her wedding ring!

Smelling coffee brewing and hearing Bismarck bark in the distance, Megan levered herself up, resting on her elbows, the sheet pulling across her breasts, partially exposing them. She saw her clothes scattered around the room, odds and ends here and there, and she remembered.

Did she ever remember! Every exquisite minute! She had never realized that a woman could feel this way about a man. She loved Alan! He loved her! She squirmed under the covers, her body tingling with remembrance, hungry again for his intimate caresses and whispers of love.

She threw the sheet aside and stood up, walking to stand

in front of the dresser, staring at her reflection for a minute or two before she turned and moved to the bathroom, adjusted the spray of the shower, remembering another morning when they had bathed together.

Reveling in the delightful memories, she let the cool water spill over her, holding her face up, exposing the long, slender column of her neck to the pricking droplets. Her eyes closed, and she stood there until she heard the door open.

"Come get it before it gets cold," Alan announced.

The freshly perked coffee enticing her, she quickly turned the taps off, wrapped a towel around herself, and stepped into the bedroom. She smiled tremulously as her fingers tucked in the towel above her left breast. He smiled triumphantly.

"I woke earlier than you, and I made us some coffee. How do you take yours?" He set the tray on the nightstand, adding sugar to his cup.

"Three sugars, no cream."

"Three sugars!" he exclaimed, turning around to glare at her. When she nodded he dropped three teaspoons of sugar into her coffee and stirred it.

She walked to the edge of the bed, watching him.

How strange it was that he knew her so well, knew her thoughts without her having to speak, knew every secret, velvety inch of her body—and didn't even know how she took her coffee. How much they still had to learn about each other. And a lifetime to learn it, she thought happily. When he held the cup out, she took it, cradling it with both hands before she sipped the hot, sweet liquid.

"Ummm," she droned appreciatively, "this tastes heavenly."

"I don't see how," he quipped dryly. "It's more like syrup than coffee." She pulled a face at him but said nothing else, and they both quietly drank their coffee.

His cup emptied, he leaned over and set it on the night-

142

stand. "Hurry up," he enjoined, "we've got lots to do and not much time to do it in." His eyes caught the whiff of lace that still lay beside the bed. His hand dropped and his fingers caught the lace, throwing the panties in Megan's lap. "You've caused enough delay as it is."

Megan looked fully into his face, her lips curving into a seductive smile. Feeling slightly lazy, in no hurry, and very much in love, she squirmed on the bed, pushing against the crumpled pillow, accepting the indictment. Slowly she finished her coffee, peeking at him over the rim. Finally she spoke, her voice full of laughter. "If I've caused delay, it was for a good reason. Not just any man could keep me in bed this long."

Rolling over close to her, his hands spanning her waist, Alan snarled, "No other man better try." He lay his head in her lap, wrapping his arms around her. After several minutes of silence, he asked, his voice pensive and serious, "Do you mind giving up your job and your freedom?"

Megan smiled reassuringly, moving slightly, her fingers playing with the rust hair. "I'm not giving up my freedom," she explained. "It's my freedom that allows me the right to choose and to make decisions. I just had to decide if I were ready for the responsibility of love and marriage."

"And?" he questioned, his voice low and quiet.

"And I was and I am," she laughed. "I'm free to love you, to follow you, and this is what I desire the most out of life."

His grip around her waist tightened. "What about giving up your job?" he persisted.

Her fingertips lightly feathered through his hair, gently kneading his scalp. "I didn't give up my job." She spoke consolingly and softly. "I just gave up my present position." She smiled when he flipped on his back and gazed up at her, furrowing his brow and squinching his eyes. "I'm excited about my transfer to Del Rio." Her fingers smoothed his brow. "Don't frown," she admonished.

"You'll age before your time." Then she smiled. "Besides, I'll enjoy learning more about the company, and I'll enjoy being an assistant store manager. Most of all," she conceded happily, "I'll be with you and Matt. I'll be with my family."

Softly Alan chuckled. "Farrell wasn't too pleased with your decision to go with me, was he?"

Megan laughed with him, remembering Farrell's surprise when in one breath she had announced her marriage and in the next had asked for a transfer. She could still see him as he chewed on the short stubby cigar and squirmed his obese form in the large swivel chair.

"No, he wasn't pleased," she replied, her mind quickly recalling the events of that Monday when she returned to work after her short vacation.

After she had told Farrell of her engagement and had asked for a transfer, he had laid his glasses on the desk, had leaned back in the chair, and had bridged his hands in front of him, resting his elbows on the arms of his chair. He stared at the woman sitting across from him. Because Megan had worked for him for the past seven years and because he liked her, he didn't hesitate to bombard her with questions: who, what, when, where, but mostly why.

When he lapsed into silence, his tirade over, Megan patiently answered all his questions but failed to reassure him about her happiness. No amount of persuasion convinced Farrell that she could find it in Los Nogalitos.

Having exhausted all arguments, he laboriously moved in his chair again, shifting his weight until he was more comfortable. "You're determined to go out there with this fellow?"

Megan grinned, nodding her head. "I'm determined."

He leaned forward, picked up his glasses, and adjusted them on his face, pushing them up on his nose. Without speaking again, he thumbed through some files that lay scattered across his desk. He twisted his mouth, pushing the cigar into the other corner, biting down on it. Through clenched teeth he said, "Richard Evers is asking for an assistant manager for his store."

Megan nodded. "I know. Would you recommend me for the position?" Her voice was calm and businesslike, coolly efficient, but Farrell could hear the plea.

Again he absently fluttered through the file, looking at but not seeing the contents. "There would be a salary adjustment in the beginning," he pointed out, his tone indicating that she would be making less than what she was making now.

"I mind," she returned evenly, "but I can accept it. Eventually I can work up again, can't I?"

Farrell nodded, taking his cigar out of his mouth, rolling it between his fingers and thumb. "Also it might necessitate occasional traveling." He saw her nod. "You know, buying, that sort of thing."

"I'd enjoy that," she admitted, "and I'm sure that Alan wouldn't mind. I might as well know the diamond business from the ground up. When we come back to Dallas, I'll be qualified for another position perhaps, a better one."

Farrell stuffed the cigar back into his mouth and grunted his acknowledgment. "When do you want to report to work?"

Now Megan hesitated. No matter how good a friend Farrell was, he was boss first, friend second. And she dreaded to ask for too much time off. Yet she wanted time for her and Matt, time for them to learn about each other, time for acceptance and adjustment.

Farrell understood her silence. He again pushed his glasses up on his nose, fiddling with them for a second before he spoke. "How much vacation do you have left?"

"Two weeks." Not much, she thought, holding her breath, waiting.

He drummed his fingers on the desk meditatively, not speaking for what seemed like an eternity to Megan.

"Could you be ready to report to work in say . . ." His voice hummed to a halt, and he quickly rifled through his looseleaf desk calendar, shoving his glasses up on his nose another time. "Let's see. A week to move . . ." Again he mumbled to himself, picking up the cigar stub and pushing it into one corner of his mouth, chewing on it, getting it firmly entrenched between his back teeth. "How much comp time?"

"A week."

He nodded, lighting a match, sticking the flame to the end of the cigar and puffing. Between puffs he asked, "How about the first of July?"

Megan grinned and squealed her delight. "Oh, Farrell, thank you," she cried.

"Don't thank me yet," he enjoined gruffly. "Wait until you've had the job for about six months, then see if you want to thank me." He peered over the rim of his glasses. "But you can handle it. I've got confidence in you. Also Dick's one of the best. You couldn't ask for a better manager or trainer."

Returning to the present, Megan gazed at the man who just this morning—just five days after her conversation with Farrell—had become her husband. Both had wanted a small service with only relatives and close friends present, so they were married in the garden at Alan's home with his mother and grandfather and a few of Megan's close friends attending. Although Megan's parents had given their blessings, they had been unable to attend the ceremony on such a short notice.

"No regrets?" Alan's gentle prodding touched the tenderness of her love for him.

"None," she replied, her fingers stroking his brow.

"You don't mind having a ready-made family?"

She grinned. "Not really. I just hope Matt loves me half as much as he loves my dog."

146

Alan chuckled. "He will. He takes after his father, and his father has excellent taste in women."

Megan's grin turned into a smile, and she softly whispered, "I love you, Alan McDonald. I love you very much."

"And I love you," he confessed, his green eyes locked with the soft gray ones. "Are you sure about our not taking a honeymoon now?"

"I'm sure," she replied, her words warmly confident. "These next few weeks are going to be crucial for Matt and me, and he needs to be included in our love." She leaned over and kissed his lips lightly. "Besides, a honeymoon is a state of mind, not a place."

"I couldn't agree more," Alan naughtily teased, his hand straying under the edge of the towel, his fingertips tickling the roundness of her bottom. "I think I'm ready for more honeymoon."

"Again?" she exclaimed with feigned affrontry.

"Again," he decried with a lecherous grin. But he didn't move. Rather, he held her in his arms for a long while, savoring the tenderness of the moment, the magnitude of her love, her willing sacrifice. Suddenly he rolled over, an impish grin playing on his mouth. "Are you planning on getting dressed today?"

With a saucy flounce, Megan rolled over too. "Of course," she announced, hopping to her feet, making sure the flap in the towel was secure. She walked to the dresser and took out clean underwear. With impudence she said, "I think I'll go into the bathroom to change."

Before she could move, however, Alan levered up and sprinted across the room. Before she realized his intentions, he caught the flap in the towel, yanking it loose.

"Oh, no, you don't." His growling laughter caused her to giggle. "This is the one part of our marriage that I enjoy very much, Megan McDonald, and I refuse to give it up."

She batted her eyes flirtatiously, her thick lashes fan-

147

ning against her cheeks, forming a dark brown crescent. "You're shocking my modesty," she declared theatrically.

Teasingly Alan leered at her, amused with her witticism. "I'll do more than shock your modesty," he warned. "There'll be no hiding things between us, especially your beautiful body." His eyes roved hungrily over her breasts.

His hands slid down her back to rest on her full hips, gently pressuring her body nearer to his. His lips lightly teased the roundness of her breasts, finally capturing one of the pink tips. She gasped with erotic pleasure, her arms winding tightly about him.

She threw the pieces of underwear she was clutching to the floor at the same time that his hands, his lips, his tongue began their sensual ravaging. Once again her body pounded for the fullness of his, and once again he was willing to comply because only she could assuage the raw hunger that gnawed within him.

He lifted her, carried her to the bed, sweeping the covers aside with one motion as she rolled over. With fluid movement his shirt was discarded, thrown to the floor, dropped with the pants, followed by his briefs, falling on top of his shoes and socks.

When he was completely undressed, he sat on the edge of the bed, staring at her with the same passion-glazed intensity that flared in her eyes. He saw her dark hair fanned around her face, her gray eyes drugged with erotic want, her pink cheeks and rosy lips, her breasts firm and uptilted, her long midriff narrowing into her waist, her hips and thighs.

Her fingers began to swirl around his navel, her nails teasing the sensitive skin, sending tremors through his body. Down the designs went, her eyes feasting on his virility, consuming her fill of his handsomeness. When he sucked in his breath, and she felt his stomach cave in, she smiled, her tongue gently tipping her top lip, coating it with shining moisture.

Unable to keep away from her, he leaned over, his hand feathering across her breasts as he rained kisses over her face, her throat, the hollow at the base of her neck. She wriggled, clutching him, drawing him nearer, but he caught her hands, pulling them above her head.

Holding them in this position, his eyes, smoldering with longing, fastened hungrily on the beautiful orbs, the tips of which were darkened from lovemaking. Slowly his head lowered, his mouth opened, his lips gently circling a hardened nipple. His tongue stroked, his mouth suckled; both played havoc with her emotions and senses, causing her to moan and writhe uncontrollably against the hard length of his body.

Expertly, lovingly, his body tormented her until her body reached that point, and she begged for total consummation.

"Please." Just one word, but it was the right one.

He heard the incoherent cry, thick with feminine desire. He felt her hot hands wandering feverishly over his body. He raised his head, and her lips found his, moving sensuously, parting his, seeking, searching, finding. His body covered hers, and their union and ecstasy became one.

She lay there, replete with love, a glow on her face, again covered only with a sheet, watching Alan as he dressed. He ran a comb through his hair, looking at her reflection in the mirror more than his. He smiled when his eyes caught hers; she smiled too.

"Don't you think it's about time you quit behaving like baggage, my sweet wife?" She grinned unabashedly. "You'd better get up and get dressed. You need something to eat before Matt gets here."

She fluffed her pillow, moving just enough that the sheet fell, partially exposing her breasts. "Doesn't the Bible say something about man not living by bread alone?" she quipped, flexing her newly acquired sexual prowess.

He laughed. "Don't start misquoting the scriptures,

dear one." He turned, leaning against the dresser, crossing his arms over his chest. "And you certainly do need something to eat, and," he drawled, "even if you don't, I do. I haven't eaten since early yesterday morning."

Deliberately she yawned and sat up, letting the sheet slowly slide down, her breasts fully exposed. Gracefully, sensuously, she lifted her arms, stretching. Alan watched each movement, gentle laughter gleaming in his green eyes.

"You almost tempt me, my darling, but not quite." He quickly moved to the side of the bed, catching her hand to pull her up. Spinning her toward her underwear, he lightly tapped her bare buttocks. "Now get dressed." But rather than release her, he eased her backward against himself. "If you don't," he promised, his voice softening to a husky whisper, "we may not get to eat for another night."

She danced away, laughing as she scurried to the pile of clothes that still lay where she had dropped them earlier. While she dressed, Alan made the bed and picked up her suit and blouse from the floor.

"What time will Matt get here?" Megan asked, running the brush through her hair.

"If they left at nine, they should pull in somewhere around six or seven." He chuckled. "Bet you never dreamed that you'd spend your honeymoon at Six Flags or Lion Country Safari."

Megan laid the brush on the dresser and walked to him, taking the skirt and blouse from his unresisting hands, slinging them on the bed. "I don't care about anything but being with you," she murmured, her body pressing closely to his. "And I certainly don't mind including Matt in our love. Love only grows and multiplies if it's shared, and we've got plenty to share." She planted quick feathery kisses on the corner of his mouth, her fingers tracing the outline as she did. "Just think of the nights after Matt's asleep."

Alan's arms closed like vises around her waist, and he buried his face in the soft curve of her neck, his lips burrowing in the thick richness of her hair. "All I think of, love, is you. Day and night." He sighed and stepped back. "If we don't get out of here right now, Meggie, I'm warning you that you might not have another chance."

Megan laughed happily, dancing out of his arms. "That isn't what you should say, Alan. That's more a delightful promise than a warning." Nonetheless, she hung up her skirt and blouse before she slipped into a pair of sandals. "Now, sir," she said, her hand motioning down the length of her body, "I'm all dressed and covered up. Surely I can't tempt you now."

"You could wear a potato sack and tempt me," Alan returned. "Remember, I'm the man who knows what's under all those clothes."

Megan grinned. "Maybe we'd better go then." She walked to the dresser and picked up her purse, slinging it over her shoulder. "I'm glad we're staying here at the apartment until we leave. This way we'll start out as a family. You, Matt, and me."

Bismarck, jealous of her new love, whined softly and nuzzled her hand.

"And Bismarck," Alan added, chuckling, fondling the dog's neck and head.

Then Alan's green eyes, which were fathomless with love and tenderness, caught and held Megan's. "I'm so glad you married me, Megan. I've been lonely for so long, and I've wanted a real family."

Love constricted her throat, and she swallowed tightly, tears glowing in her eyes. "You won't be lonely again, darling." Softly she asked, moving into the protective shelter of his arms, "What if our family's already begun to grow?"

Alan stared at her for a full second before he understood. Then he smiled. "I don't mind," he finally admitted before he added, "Guess I hadn't given it too much thought. But I hope not for a little while. Somewhere between kids I'd like to have you to myself, and I'd like for us to take a real honeymoon."

"We will," Megan promised, "in between babies." Then she laughed joyously. "I'm so happy, Alan. So happy that I'm almost afraid."

"What's there to be afraid of?" he asked, his arms tightening around her, pulling her closer yet.

"I don't know," she mumbled against his chest. "Matt maybe; Elena maybe." She drew a deep breath. "Your memories of Linda maybe."

He made no comment; he just held her tightly. "Don't be afraid," he eventually enjoined softly. "Our love's strong enough to conquer all fear, whether it's real or imagined." He whispered into the shining strands of her hair. "I love you, and you love me. That's what counts."

Her face brushed up and down on his chest as she nodded.

# CHAPTER SEVEN

"A barbecue dinner for the entire community of Los Nogalitos!" Megan had gasped, her eyes wide with disbelief. "Cooking TV dinners is my speed. I don't think I can handle an affair this big."

"Of course, you can," Alan had said dismissively. "After all, George, Rosa, and I will be here to help you."

That had been last Saturday as they drove home from Dallas. Now on this beautiful Saturday morning four weeks after their marriage, Megan and Alan with the help of Rosa and George were scurrying about in the backyard preparing for the barbecue dinner at which Alan planned to introduce Megan to his friends and neighbors. Megan and Rosa had cooked pounds of beans and potatoes and were now mixing the potato salad. Alan and George had been erecting spits over the back lawn for the barbecueing of the beef and pork.

During the first opportunity for a break, Alan took Megan into the kitchen, poured them large glasses of iced tea, and then led her to the study. Both of them gladly collapsed on the brown leather sofa, gulping their tea.

"I'm glad Rosa took Matt with her," Alan sighed. "I'm too tired to keep up with the skimp."

Megan chuckled. "But Rosa isn't."

Alan laughed with her, catching her hand, pulling her closer to him. "She asked for him, and she got him." Then his lips curved into that maddening grin. "I don't think she's as fond of Bismarck, but she got him too." He took Megan's empty glass and set it on the coffee table. Leaning back, he folded her into his arms. "Happy fourth-week anniversary, darling."

"I'm glad you remembered," Megan retorted pertly. "I thought you were taking me for granted and had forgotten."

"No, indeed," Alan countered heartily. "You're the most valuable asset in my life. I couldn't afford to take you for granted."

"I'm glad," Megan murmured, suddenly quite serious.

"In fact, I've got an anniversary present for you," he announced. "One that I've been working on for some time now."

"A present," she shrieked delightedly. "A present for me? What is it?"

Alan chuckled contentedly, sighing deeply, his fingers playing with the silken strands of hair that fell against his chest. "What do you think about our building your dream house?"

"My house," she squealed. "My house! You're going to build my house!"

Alan shook his head in gentle amusement. "How about *our* house? You know, I plan to live in it too."

"Our house." Megan corrected herself willingly on a long sigh.

"The manager's house is hardly large enough for both Rosa and George, and there's certainly no room for Matt, much less Bismarck, so . . ." he droned, his tone light and playful, "if we plan on using them as baby-sitters and if

154

we plan to let them manage the farm when we eventually return to Dallas, we'd better make sure they have a house to live in. Right?"

"Right," Megan concurred, her mind racing miles ahead of him. "So we'll build the new house for us and let George and Rosa have this one?"

"That's right," Alan agreed. "We'll have our own house, and we'll start our own memories."

"Oh, Alan," Megan breathed ecstatically, "I'm all for it." She pressed her lips to his cheek, saying in a muffled voice, "It's beautiful, Alan. Thank you very much."

Alan suddenly levered up from the sofa, catching her hand and pulling her with him. "Come here just a minute," he said, moving toward the desk. He leaned down, opened the bottom drawer, and took out a brown portfolio which was worn with use. Untying the string, he pulled out a sheaf of papers, handing one to Megan.

"Look at this," he said. "See if you like it."

With trembling hands she took the sketch and looked at it. Her eyes were shining and bright with anticipation. "Oh, Alan," she murmured her pleasure, "this is exactly what I've dreamed about. This *is* my house, isn't it?" Her eyes misted with tears of happiness. "You drew these sketches up from my description, didn't you?" He didn't answer, but she didn't notice. She continued to look at the drawing and talk. "The red-tiled roof, the adobe look, the Spanish hacienda." She threw the sheet of paper on the desk and wrapped both her arms around Alan, hugging him tightly. "I love you so much."

"And I love you," he returned, pecking light kisses on her nose. "I take it that you're pleased with the drawings."

"More than pleased," she returned. "I'm ecstatic over them. How soon will it be before we can start building?"

He laughed and roughed up her hair. "Tonight a close friend of mine, Ric Alvarez, will be coming to the barbecue. He's an architect, and among the three of us we're going to put the finishing touches to our plans, and he'll draft the blueprints."

"Oh, Alan," Megan squealed, at a loss for any other words, her happiness bubbling over.

He stepped back, picked up another packet of papers, and carefully unfolded them, pressing them flat on the desk. "These are photostatic copies of pages from a diary written by a Spanish officer who was stationed in America during the 1700s. Although he never identifies the hacienda by more than Hacienda del Lago, from the locations and towns he cites I have reason to believe that he stayed at our hacienda." His finger hit several excerpts that were marked with red ink. "Look at the translations here in the margin. He describes the entire house, colors, types of furniture, wall decorations, and here"—hurriedly he flipped through the pages—"he states that from the master bedroom, which overlooked the lake, one could see the beautiful sunrise each morning."

Again Megan crooned, "Oh, Alan, how romantic! How gorgeous! How did you get all of this?" she demanded, her mind agog with excitement, her words tumbling out. "When did you begin all this research? Why did you start it?"

Alan laughed. "One question at a time, please. I started the research years ago when I first bought the property." He hesitated, but Megan was too enthralled with his story to notice, and as he talked she thumbed through the pages of the diary, scanning the interpretation in the margin.

"I guess you might say," he continued, "that I began out of, ah, curiosity, and then I really got involved with it, entranced by its beauty and magnitude. Next I managed to convert Ric to my enthusiasm, and he started helping me gather information. Wanting to specialize in Spanish designs, he made several trips to Spain, and he enticed the curators—lovely señoritas in most cases—at the archives to help him uncover all this material that I now have." Alan threw his head back and laughed. "I can only imagine what else he uncovered during all this research, and I doubt that it was all history."

Megan chuckled as Alan briefly gave her a physical and character description of his close friend. By the time Alan had completed his tale, Megan was laughing until tears moistened her eyes, and she felt as if she knew the tall, tan-complexioned man with the smoky brown eyes.

"Ric has a certain persuasive charm that captivates the most beautiful," Alan concluded. "I'm telling you all this because I don't want you to succumb to his spell."

"Don't worry, sweetheart," Megan murmured, moving back to the warmth of his chest. "You have me completely under your spell." Silently she nestled for a long time, savoring the beauty and joy of the moment. "I've always wanted to be a part of something like this," she dreamily asserted. "I feel like I'm part of history, as if we're turning the pages of time back."

"This isn't all," Alan said, leaning down, pulling on another drawer. "Look at these," he said, opening the file that he had taken out. He handed Megan some pen-and-ink drawings and while she looked at them he tapped some small photos from the file jacket. "When Ric was in Mexico City, studying at the university, he told his professor about our hacienda, and the professor pointed out this painting that was titled "Hacienda del Lago"—a painting, by the way, with no history and no name, just a date in a far corner. Ric was captured by its beauty, but he was also positive that it was our El Lago Lindo. Pulling some strings, the professor was allowed to take these photos, and Ric worked on his drawings from them. He sketched in the other views from information in the journal."

"Fantastic! Simply fantastic," Megan cried out, and for the next hour they sat in the study, talking about their house, decorating it, buying furniture for it, landscaping

157

it, loving it, quickly transforming it from a house to a home. But their moments were short-lived. They heard a loud commotion and above that George's gruff bellowing.

"The kegs of beer have arrived. Where do you want me to put them?"

From that moment on, a flurry of activity began that was unending. The musicians arrived, and the people began to file in. Not only did Megan meet the neighbors, but the majority of them brought gifts and dishes of their favorite foods, each person who prepared a dish kindly giving Megan the recipe and the history of it. Never in her life had she tasted so much delicious food, shaken so many hands, or exchanged as many recipes. But she was happy. Alan's friends and neighbors liked her, and she liked them.

Later in the evening, after all the people were served, Megan slipped into the house. Walking through the kitchen, she stopped long enough to pour herself a glass of tea and then trudged into the study to flop into the nearest chair. She was too exhausted even to turn on the light. She slipped her shoes off and lifted her feet, propping them on the ottoman.

She could still hear the strains of the country-western music as it drifted in, and she heard the soft drone of voices as the crowd milled around. But the fanfares were over, the meal served, and the people were happy, contented with the present company, their food, and their beer.

She was sitting in the study in her dream world, priding herself on a job well done, when suddenly the door flew open and the light flicked on. Megan turned her head, blinking several times at the effusion of brightness. She couldn't believe her eyes. Elena Mendoza, devastatingly beautiful as always, stood there. *Maybe if I sit still,* Megan thought, *close my eyes, and count to ten, she'll disappear.*

She didn't however. Instead, she arrogantly swayed into the room, clumsily groping her way to the couch that nestled in front of the chair. In her left hand she held a wineglass that was filled to the brim with champagne, drops running over and down the sides of the glass.

"You'll have to excuse me, Mrs. McDonald," she slurred sarcastically, "I've been celebrating longer than most of these folks, so I'm closer to being drunk than they are." Her voice was cracked and brittle, but she managed a croaky laugh. "Didn't expect me, did you?"

"Not really," Megan returned dryly, wishing she hadn't come, not knowing how to handle her.

"Couldn't expect me to stay away forever, could you?"

Megan shook her head. No, she thought, that was too good to hope for. But she had hoped for a longer period of time without her appearance. "Did the Burnets get tired of you?"

Elena laughed. "Nope," she sputtered on a swallow of champagne, and put the glass on a table. "I got tired of them, but"—she twirled around, landing on the couch— "I can't stay with Mom." She lifted her hand in the air, making awkward motions with her fingers. "Have you seen the little box she and George are living in? Hardly room for two, much less three."

"That'll soon change," Megan returned conversationally.

"Should," Elena replied, quickly forgetting her trend of thought. She held her glass up in the air, looking at the liquor through the gleam of the lightbulb. "Filled to the brim."

"Sounds like you are too," Megan quipped dryly, wishing Elena hadn't come, wishing she had stayed away a little longer. She had been glad to learn on her return as Mrs. Alan McDonald that Elena was staying with close friends until Rosa and George could get a bigger house.

"Probably am," Elena sniggered, enjoying the joke. "But I'm not celebrating like everybody else is. I'm in mourning." She leaned forward, speaking slowly so that her words were clearly enunciated. "When I learned that Alan had married a nobody like you, I could have died."

"Well, well," Megan purred, deceitfully sweet, "how kind of you, Elena. I'm glad to know you think so highly of me. It'll make our future dealings so much simpler."

Elena, however, ignored Megan's little tirade. "Alan's announcement also took me by surprise," she slurred, leaning back once again, "but it shouldn't have." She giggled. "I should have known that Alan was prepared to go to any lengths . . ." She deliberately let her voice trail into silence, hoping to agitate Megan into a stormy outburst.

"Look, Elena," Megan quietly said, "I'm tired, and I'm not up to your games. Neither am I interested in your drunken prattlings."

Megan's words weren't exactly a vocal extension of her thoughts. Inside she was tense, tightly coiled, ready to spring loose at any moment. She had seen that mask of bitter hatred that settled on Elena's face when Alan announced that they were going to build their home by El Lago Lindo and that they were going to reconstruct the hacienda.

"I wonder if you'll think it's drunken prattling when I get through." She threw her head back and laughed. "I didn't think Alan would have to carry things this far." She smiled, her teeth gleaming a beautiful white. "I had believed that he would find some other way."

Naturally Megan's curiosity was whetted, but she didn't question Elena's declaration. She just sat quietly. Years of training and discipline had taught her to keep a blank face, never letting the adversary know what she was thinking.

"You know what I mean?" Elena finally forced herself to ask, leaning forward, peering into Megan's closed face.

Megan smiled and said with caustic sweetness, "Sorry,

although I do have the ability to read minds, I don't make it a habit. Too much trash, you know." She laughed.

Elena glared at her but didn't immediately retort. Rather, she said, "I'm speaking about the lake property."

Megan bristled, not really knowing why, but knowing that Elena was preparing for battle, not a skirmish, but a battle of life and death.

"Sorry, again," Megan murmured coolly, "I still don't know what you mean. Guess you're going to have to explain."

Elena laughed, tipped her glass, and drank deeply of the bubbly liquid. "Alan married you for the sole reason"—she paused, an eloquently dramatic pause, raised her glass, and swirled it around in the air. "Alan married you because"—again the touch of the dramatic—"because . . . he wanted the lake property."

Megan forced herself to sit still, forced herself to look relaxed and amused. *Don't let her get to you,* she reminded herself. *That's her game. Keep her guessing! That's the only way you can win.*

"Think what you will," Megan replied, looking into her glass. With a genuine smile of amusement quirking her lips, Megan stared at Elena and continued. "I happen to know that Alan and I married because we love one another."

"Maybe you love Alan," Elena countered tormentingly, "but that doesn't necessarily mean that Alan loves you." She smiled, kicking out of her shoes, curling up in the corner of the sofa. "Maybe that's what Alan's told you." Her brows rose, and she gave Megan one of those holier-than-thou looks. "You know, some people, Megan, will say or do anything to get what they want."

Megan looked as vacuous as she could and returned Elena's stare. She managed to bite her tongue, to hold back her sharp reply. She had been taught to play the waiting game, and she'd wait. She refused to give Elena any points. She'd have to fight for any that she got.

"I'm sure that Alan loves me." Quiet assurance flowed with the words.

"No," Elena negated as firmly, lifting her hand in another grand flourish. "Alan doesn't love you. He still loves Linda." Hateful malice underlined each deliberate word. "He has never loved you, nor will he ever," Elena spit vindictively. "He has always loved Linda."

"I'm sure that Alan will never love me like he loved Linda," Megan conceded with grace, "and I wouldn't want him to." She could hardly think straight. How long ago was it that she voiced her fears to Alan! She had subconsciously feared a scene like this with Elena. She had feared the ghost of Linda Mendoza McDonald. "I'm not Linda. I'm Megan, and I deserve to be loved for myself. But I do know that Alan loves me." She pointed to herself, jabbing her index finger into her chest. "Alan loves me, Megan Jonas McDonald. And nothing you say will change it."

"You think not?" Elena chuckled, enjoying Megan's irritation. "Well, let's see, shall we? One, we know for a fact that Alan couldn't get the lake property from Joel. Two, we know for a fact that you and Alan are going to reconstruct the Hacienda del Lago Lindo on the lake property." Elena stopped, took a breath, and continued with her well-rehearsed outline. "Three, I know for a fact that Alan promised Linda that he would rebuild the hacienda by the lake for her." Gloatingly she taunted, "Not for you, Megan, but for Linda."

The pronouncement, like a death sentence, hung in the air, suspended between the two of them. Megan slowly raised the glass to her lips, sipped the tea, but didn't taste it, and swallowed.

"I once heard Joel tell Alan that the only way he'd get

the lake property from him was to marry you." She giggled. "Looks like Alan took him at his word, doesn't it?"

"He still doesn't have the property," Megan countered.

"I think so," Elena refuted. "When Alan talked to Joel on the phone, he told Joel that the two of you were married and that he wanted to build you the hacienda on the lake." She laughed with bitter amusement. "Joel gave you and Alan the property as your wedding present, Megan."

The words, like a knife, sliced into Megan's heart, but she showed no pain or anguish. "How do you know all this?" she asked.

"I overheard George and Mom talking about it," Elena admitted without shame. She tipped her glass, draining it of all liquid. Then she smacked her lips appreciatively. "How does it feel to know that you've been had, Megan?"

*Horrible,* Megan thought, a bitter taste in her mouth.

"I'm not sure that I've been *had* as you put it," she answered, her heart palpitating erratically at the thought of Alan's having used her, despair washing in on her in such waves that she felt like she was drowning.

"Alan McDonald, wealthy playboy and heir to Glynn's millions! Come on, Megan! Why should he marry a little nobody like you?" The thoughts weren't new to Megan. They had been haunting her for several weeks. "Why would Alan McDonald rush you into marriage? Insist on marriage?"

Although Megan was indignant, she also questioned Alan's motives. Why had he rushed her into marriage? Why had he chosen her when he could have had his choice of so many? Somewhere among the chaotic thoughts in her mind, Megan latched onto one. She recalled Alan's words to her that day on the lake. He had promised her that he would get the property. Obtaining it was a major goal in his life. Had he—would he—use her like this?

Elena saw the consternation on Megan's countenance

163

and seized the opportunity, continuing to twist the knife of doubt and anguish deeply into Megan's heart.

"The hacienda isn't for you, Megan. He's building it because he promised Linda that he would. It's her dream that he's fulfilling, Megan, not yours."

Over and over the words reverberated in Megan's head, the noise getting louder and louder. Still she managed to hold her outward composure. "Look," she stormed. She didn't, however, let her voice rise one iota in volumne. "Linda is dead." She slowly spelled the word. "D-E-A-D. And I'm alive. And I'm Alan's wife, no matter what the reason. And I intend to remain his wife. Do you understand me? You nor anyone else is going to run me away. Alan and I are going to be happy."

"Really?" Elena asked calmly. "Did he ever tell you that he spent the last two weeks of Linda's life with her? That they would have gone back together if she hadn't died?"

Alan's told me precious little about Linda, Megan thought grimly, anger seeping through her body. But she wasn't going to let Elena know. "He's told me about Linda." She evaded the question truthfully.

Elena nodded. "Alan never left her bedside. For two weeks, day and night, Alan stayed with her," Elena taunted.

Softly Megan answered, "I can understand that. She was dying. Of course Alan would stay. That's the sort of person he is."

Then Elena reminisced, her mind in the past, oblivious to people or things. "Linda and Alan began to study about the hacienda." She laughed, a sad, melancholy sound that tore Megan's heart in two. "We'd always been told about the hacienda, but we weren't sure that it had ever existed. It was just a story that we handed down from generation to generation." Her eyes were distant and cloudy with remembrances. "Linda always promised Poppa that she'd buy the property and build a grand hacienda."

She rose to her feet, swaying, almost falling before she could finally stand upright. "Then when Linda went back to Alan, she made him buy property out here, and they began to research the legend." She staggered to the desk, pulling out a drawer, dragging out the familiar brown packet. She untied it, dumped all the contents on the desk, and flipped through until she found the sheet that she wanted. "Look at this," she slurred, returning to Megan's chair. "What more proof do you want? This sketch has Linda's name and the year on it."

Megan took the paper that Elena held out, commanding her arms and hands to stop trembling. She turned the paper over and stared at the black-inked drawing. She saw the date in the corner; she saw the signature. There was hardly room for doubt, hardly, Megan thought, a glimmer of hope shining in the narrow space.

Elena misunderstood Megan's silence.

"I hate to be the one who had to tell you this, Megan," she lied sarcastically, "but . . ."

Alan's words thundered through the room, fury echoing in the very sound. The booming of thunder couldn't have startled the women more.

"But what?" Both women turned and looked at Alan in stunned surprise. "Tell me more, Elena. I'd like to hear it too."

Although Elena was startled, Alan noted that she was either too drunk to care or she was too bitter to exercise caution. For either reason, she quickly recovered her aplomb.

"I was telling Megan that you and Linda planned to rebuild the Hacienda del Lago Lindo years ago." She smiled, proud of herself, and she openly gloated. "I also told her that you spent the last two weeks of Linda's life with her. You remember?"

Alan walked to the desk, his lips pressed together in controlled rage. He picked up all the papers and shuffled them into the portfolio.

"Alan," Elena said, her voice a trifle wobbly, but still audacious, "do you remember Joel's telling you that the only way you'd finagle the property from him would be to marry his granddaughter."

Deliberately Alan walked to where Megan sat with the paper in her hand. "I'll take this," he said, jerking the drawing from her unresisting fingers, "and I'll give it to Ric." As he said this, however, he wadded the sheet of paper that Megan had been holding and tossed it into the wastepaper basket. He turned to Elena, and Megan saw the menacing expression on his face, and she heard the roaring anger when he spoke to Elena. "Get out of here right now, and don't come back until you can apologize to my wife for your insults and insinuations."

Elena turned and moved toward the door, stopping in the middle of the room. "Can you deny anything I've told Megan?"

"I don't have to deny or affirm anything," Alan retorted, "especially to you."

"We're not talking about me," Elena threw back as quickly. "I want to know if you can explain away these doubts to Megan's satisfaction." Elena twirled around a time or two and giggled as she stumbled across the floor in the direction of the door. "Oh, but you will, Alan," she taunted. "Megan's going to wonder the rest of her life, and I've told her the truth."

Alan glanced at Megan, who hadn't moved since he'd been in the room. Briefly, but carefully, his eyes had rushed from her head to her toes, and he knew she was in a state of shock. What had Elena told her? How much did Megan believe? Could he repair the damage?

As the questions burned in his mind, he tried to think, but he was too distraught, too angry, too concerned. He

166

wanted to throttle Elena for having stirred up this mischief. Alan took a step toward Elena, but she divined his intentions, and she clumsily ran toward the doorway, leaving her shoes behind.

"You'll never get an apology from me, Alan McDonald. I've told Megan the truth, and I'm not sorry." Then she sang the taunt, "But you will be."

Alan gave her one more glowering stare. "Elena, get out of here." He moved to the couch, leaned down, and picked up her shoes. Tossing them in her direction, he said, "Get out of here, and don't come back until you can apologize for your rudeness."

Elena wavered to her shoes, picked them up, and giggled. She turned her glass upside down. "It's empty. Guess I'll go fill it up again. I don't want to be sober for days." She staggered to the door, holding the frame with one hand, swinging around with the other hand. "Ta-ta, Megan. Here's wishing you one helluva marriage." She slammed the door behind her.

Her crowning closure, however, fell on deaf ears. Alan had turned his back on her and was moving in Megan's direction. He didn't care what Elena did or said about him, but he was concerned about its effect on Megan. His green eyes, clouded with anxiety, flitted over his wife, her pallor, the tense quietness, the tear-glazed eyes.

"Megan." He knelt beside the chair, taking her hands into his, setting her glass on the floor. He softly rubbed her cold hands with his warm ones. "Megan," he implored again. "Look at me."

Slowly, as if she were a robot following his command, she looked at him, her face void of expression, a stunned resignation glinting in her eyes. He wasn't sure if she saw him or not. Her eyes registered no recognition, nor did they emit signals of censure. They said nothing. Anything would have been preferable to this, he thought.

His voice softened, the husky strains meant to be soothing and caressive. "Megan, tell me what Elena said that's upset you."

Without thinking, but so slowly that it appeared a deliberate strategy, Megan extracted her hands from his and rubbed them together. Then she smiled, that old curving of the lips that never reached the eyes, that hollow smile that hid the soul of the woman whom he loved. Her eyes flicked over her hands, which she held together very composedly in her lap.

"I believe Elena hit all the major points," Megan answered, adding, "She must have done quite well in her speech classes—enumerate her main points, explain them, then summarize them."

Alan grasped her shoulders in a tight grip, not realizing that he was hurting her. Shaking her, he said, "Megan, come out of it. You're in a state of shock."

Megan winced and grimaced from the pain, but it did jolt her back to reality, and it ended the numbed shock that had encased her heart and emotions. Now anger, frustration, hurt, anguish, and fear—yes, fear, most of all, raged through her—all merging together to form a clot that wouldn't pass through her heart, stopping the flow of blood and thought, stopping the air from reaching her lungs.

The drumming sound was getting louder and louder; she thought she would pass out. She needed to get a gasp of fresh air. She needed—she didn't know what she needed. But she knew what she wanted. She wanted Alan to deny the accusations. She wanted him to convince her that she was the one who mattered, not Linda.

Through the horrific clamor of thoughts that whirlwinded through Megan's mind, she heard herself say, "Wouldn't you be in a state of shock if you'd just heard someone accuse the person you love of deceit?"

"Megan—" Alan could say no more. Megan turned her cold, gunmetal gray eyes on him and shot him to the heart.

"Have you talked with Gramps recently?"

"Megan." Alan tried to placate her quietly. "Let's talk about this later. A yes or no is impossible. You won't understand."

Tears shimmered in her eyes, but her voice was strong and even. "You talked with Gramps and didn't tell me?"

He nodded his head. "Megan, please let's talk about this later. I came to get you because the people are asking about you. We need to get back to them." His eyes pleaded with her for understanding. "I promise that I'll discuss this with you."

"Did you and Gramps discuss the property, Alan? Did you ask him to deed us the property now that we were married?"

"Do you think so little of me?" Alan exploded, anxious and frustrated, not knowing how to deal with this side of Megan, not having ever seen it before. Also he felt the hot rage of anger as it flamed through his body. How could she doubt his love for her? How could such a little issue become so paramount as to be a measure of his love for her?

"I don't know what I think," Megan returned truthfully, her hands fluttering to her hair, her fingers taking out the combs. "I just want to know if you reminded Gramps of his promise. Did you ask him for the property now that we were married?" She combed her hair and reinserted the combs. "Yes or no, Alan."

Reluctantly Alan nodded, afraid of her reaction, afraid because she didn't know the entire story. "I told your grandfather that we were married, and I wanted to build our house by the lake." Alan paused. "I reminded him of his promise."

No visible reaction! Megan continued to stare, her thoughts a mystery even to her. Her voice was so low that Alan could hardly hear her when she spoke. "Did you

169

promise Linda on her deathbed that you would buy all the Mateo y Mendoza property back for her?"

"Megan," he pleaded with exasperation, "please wait!"

"Did you?" came the hoarse insistence. "I want to know."

"I did." A soft, truthful confession, wrung out of him.

"Did Gramps promise you that the property would be deeded to my husband and me in an effort to get you to marry me?"

The pallor in her expression was nothing to match the deathlike tones of her question. Alan knew what she was asking, and he wished he could give her the explanations and comforting she needed, but he could hear the people getting rowdy and rambunctious. He needed to be there with them. He needed to be here with her.

"Don't be silly," he vociferated. "You should know both your grandfather and me better than that. Joel was joking. True, I married you knowing that Joel would give us the property, but I didn't marry you for that land!"

Megan brushed past him, slowly walking to the window, staring blindly outside. "You didn't draw the sketches from my description." Her voice was hollow and dead. "You—" She inhaled deeply, but her voice when she continued to speak was strong and without emotion. "You already had them, didn't you?" She wanted no answer; she wanted to think aloud. She wanted to rid her heart of this grief before it festered and formed a raw, running sore. She lifted her hand, rubbing her cheek and temple. "You were fulfilling another woman's dream, weren't you?" She tried to laugh, but the sound was more like a bitter snort than laughter. "Elena was right. I came along at the right time, and I was ripe for the plucking."

Somewhere in the distance she heard a door open and slam; she heard the heavy footsteps in the hall; she heard the heavy pounding on the door.

"Alan."

She heard George's rough voice.

"This barbecue was given in honor of you and Megan. I think the least you two can do is join us. People are asking about you."

"Okay, George," Alan called, never moving, his eyes never wavering from Megan. Softly he refuted Megan's statement. "That's not true, Megan."

He took the two or three strides and he stood behind her. But when his hands touched her shoulders, she flinched them aside.

"Like Shane you wanted me while you could use me. You wanted me because you could use me."

Again the pounding on the door. "Are you two gonna come or not?"

"We're coming, George," Alan returned, a little more sharply this time. "Give me about ten more minutes." Alan was more concerned about the raw and ragged anguish that was cutting Megan apart than he was the crowd outside.

"No, Megan," he argued gently, "that's not true either, and if you'll think for a few minutes, you'll admit it. You know that I love you." He slowly lifted his hands, wondering if he dared touch her again, knowing only that he had to touch her, he had to reach her. Ever so tenderly, the palms of his hands touched her shoulders, softly the fingers closed a bit. "Please give me a chance to explain, to vindicate myself."

This time it was Rosa's voice that called through the thickness of the door. "The people are waiting. They want to begin the dancing, and the first dance should be yours."

"Please," Alan whispered, waiting for her answer. To Rosa he said, "Be right out."

Megan heard the gentle concern and anxiety. She sensed Alan's despair. "Okay," she whispered, nodding, not adding anything more.

"Megan, I love you." He wanted the same declaration

171

from her. Never had he been so vulnerable; never had he wanted reassurance like he wanted it now.

She only nodded, not speaking because she knew she would start crying, and she wasn't ready for an emotional outpouring at the moment. There were the guests to consider; there were George and Rosa; there was Matt. Too many people, too much was at stake tonight. She had to keep a tight grip on her emotions.

Alan misunderstood. His hands gripped her shoulders tighter, and he twirled her around. "Megan," he cried, hopelessness causing him to sound harsh and angry, "surely you don't accept Elena's accusations as gospel truth? Surely you're going to let me explain?"

## CHAPTER EIGHT

Alan walked through the house, switching off the lights in each room as he moved toward the bedroom. He was worried about Megan. Ever since they'd returned to the barbecue she'd been quiet and withdrawn, coolly polite but definitely preoccupied with her own thoughts. Now he had the difficult task of explaining away all those lies that Elena had told her.

Wearily he opened and closed the door to the bedroom, fully expecting to find Megan there, but the room was empty. Only the muted light of the bed lamp splaying across the thick carpet gave evidence of life in the room. Alan walked to the rocker which still swayed gently back and forth. He picked up the skirt and scarf she'd been wearing. He stood still, listening, looking around. Perhaps she was taking a bath, even though he couldn't hear the water.

"Megan," he called, dropping the clothes, walking to the bathroom. "Are you in here?" At the same time that he asked the question, he opened the door and peered into the room. No Megan! Not a sign of Megan!

He returned to the bedroom, wondering where she

could be. She'd been with him when the Fowlers left. They were the last, weren't they? She'd been with him when Rosa and George had asked if Matt could spend the night with them. Where could she be now? What could she be doing?

He wrenched the door open, walked down the hall calling for her, but received no answer. As he searched each room he left the light on, his bewilderment growing with each passing second. He strode across the living room then sprinted up the steps into the kitchen. He checked the note pad by the telephone, but there was no message.

Then he heard that soft sound, the sound of a car door slamming. In that split-second he galvanized into action, dashing out of the house, racing toward the garage. He feared that Megan was leaving. He'd known that she was upset, but he hadn't reckoned on this. *Dear God*, he fervently supplicated, *don't let her leave me.*

*God, she couldn't leave me,* he thought. *She couldn't! Not without giving me a chance to explain.* Then he lifted his head. He saw her. She was standing by her car, holding a suitcase in her hands. Thank God, he'd reached her before she left.

He was by her side in a second, his hands biting into her wrist. Megan turned startled gray eyes on him, dropping her valise. "Alan," she cried, wincing from his grip, "turn me loose. You're hurting me."

"I'll turn you every way but loose," he snapped, his anger obscuring rational thought for the moment. "How dare you try to run away! How childish! Dear God, Megan," he exploded, "why couldn't you wait for my explanation?" With every word he took a step in the direction of the house, dragging her all the way.

"Alan," she pleaded, resisting him, "let me get my suitcase." She couldn't understand his anger. "I don't want to leave it out here."

174

"I couldn't care less about your suitcase," he barked, never slowing down, never looking around.

"Well, I do," she shouted in return, both hands trying to pry his loose. "That's my new lingerie, and I don't intend to leave it out here."

Ignoring her outburst, Alan said, "One woman ran away from me, one woman ran out on my child, but I swore that I would never lose another wife, and I promised myself that Matt would never lose another mother."

"I wasn't running away," Megan snapped, her feet tangling in the monkey grass by the sidewalk, causing her to stumble. "I was merely—"

"You weren't, were you?" Alan questioned mockingly. "Why did you slip out of the house? Why the suitcase? Why at your car at this time of the morning? Do you always undress out here?"

"Oh, Alan," Megan almost laughed, her hands still clawing at his fingers which felt like they were entrenched several inches in her flesh. "Don't be ridiculous!"

"Don't be ridiculous!" he fulminated. "Are you referring to me?"

"Oh, Alan," she laughed, still struggling with him. "I don't mean that you're ridiculous. You're just—you're just acting childish."

"I'm so angry that I could gladly whip you," he stormed.

"Don't you dare," she sputtered, all amusement wiped from her face. "Being jealous is one thing, but I don't intend to be treated like a child. And I don't like being hauled over the lawn like a sack of potatoes. At least turn me loose and let me walk by your side in a dignified manner."

Not listening to her, his thoughts hammering too loudly, fear of losing her still coursing through his bloodstream, he stopped and stared into her face, which he

175

could see clearly in the moonlight. His words thundered through the early morning silence with harshness.

"Remember this, Megan McDonald. I never ran after Linda. Not one time. And I won't run after you again. I love you, and I don't want to lose you, but I won't spend my life chasing after you. If you live with me, you'll do it of your own free will because you love and trust me." Megan could hear the truth of his promise.

Then, and only then, did he release her, spinning on his heels as soon as he'd finished speaking and walking into the house, leaving her standing speechless on the walk. Slowly she shook her head, rubbing her wrist where his fingers had so recently been, collected her wits and her humor, and went back for her suitcase.

He stood in the kitchen door, his expression taut and apprehensive, waiting. He watched her every movement, poised, ready to go after her if she failed to return to him. Megan could feel the tenseness as she walked through the door.

"I wasn't running away," she explained softly. "And I was waiting for your explanation."

His head dipped once, but Megan couldn't tell if he believed her or not, and she didn't have time to question him because he started talking and walking again. She had to run to keep up with him.

"Linda ran off and left Matt when he was a tiny baby, and I hated her for that. I never forgave her for deserting him when he was so sick and so helpless. Rosa and I were up with him day and night for weeks before his fever completely broke, but Linda couldn't have cared less."

"Alan," Megan gasped, tottering more than walking behind him down the hallway, her suitcase bouncing against her legs, causing her to be unsteady. "How many times must I tell you, I wasn't running away. I went to the car to get my lingerie." She stopped, threw the case on the floor and knelt. "Here," she shouted, "I want you to see."

176

With fumbling fingers she unlocked the case, lifted the lid, and threw her beautiful underwear and nightgowns over the hall. "See, Alan, I went to get one of my new sexy nightgowns to sleep in, to tempt you with."

In spite of his anger and fear, Alan grinned, looking down at the indignant woman at his feet. He hardly glanced at the filmy clothing strewn all about. Casually he leaned against the doorframe of their bedroom and folded his arms over his chest.

"We didn't get this one when we unpacked," Megan finished, her voice lowered, all anger evaporated. She grabbed her clothes and stuffed them into the case but didn't have a chance to close it.

Alan knelt beside her, slammed the lid down, and picked it up with one hand, holding the other out for Megan. "Here," he said quietly, his anger gone too, "let me help you." Together they went into the bedroom, and he set the case on the antique love seat that stood at the end of their bed. He turned, looked at Megan, and caught her other hand in his. He gently tugged it, and she willingly fell into the safety of his arms.

"I knew by the time that Linda ran off that she didn't love me, but I had thought she would love her child." His grip tightened, and Megan could feel his hurt and anguish. "I promised myself that if I ever remarried, it would be to a woman who loved me, Megan, not my money or my position, one who would stick by me through thick and thin. I promised myself that I would marry a woman who would love my son and who would love giving me other sons and daughters and who would love them with me."

"That's the only reason you rushed me into marriage?" she asked, glowing with the knowledge that he loved her, had chosen her over all other women, loved her over all other women.

He slowly eased her out of his arms, gazing down at her, eating and drinking his fill of her unpretentious loveliness.

He nodded. "That's why I rushed you into marriage, Megan. I was afraid of losing you, and I loved you too much to risk losing you." Feeling vulnerable, he turned and walked to the window, quietly looking at the now empty lawn. With his back to her, he placed both hands on his hips, hooking his thumbs in the back pockets of his jeans.

"I'm sorry that Elena hurt you."

Megan hardly dared move. She didn't want to break the sweetness of the moment. Now she knew; now she understood. Her husband's anger hadn't been directed toward her. It was an anger born of fear. He feared her leaving him. He had once known the naked loneliness of being deserted, and she knew that he didn't want to feel it again. As much as she needed his love, she realized, he needed hers. As much as she wanted his reassurance, he wanted hers.

"She tried to hurt me," Megan corrected, now moving closer to him. "She tried, but she didn't succeed."

Still he didn't turn. "But you believed her!" Not a question, but a bald statement of fact.

At the moment when she and Alan had been standing in the study, immediately after Elena's accusations, Megan hadn't known whether she believed Elena or not. At that precise moment she had been sure of only one thing: She loved Alan. Her love for him had never wavered. She had never doubted his love for her. There had been that small glimmer of hope.

Probably what had concerned her the most and had preoccupied her thoughts was the sense of betrayal she had felt. She had trusted Alan blindly; she had trusted Gramps implicitly. Yet both of them—the two people whom she trusted and loved the most—had betrayed her, so she thought. Whether it was for a good reason or not, both of them had deceived her. Alan had asked for the title to the property without consulting her, and Gramps had agreed to give it to him without a word to her. Naturally she was hurt because Alan didn't tell her.

Alan turned now, his hands resting on the top button of his shirt. Again his words broke the tense silence.

"You believed her!"

Megan stood, not speaking because she was suddenly filled with an unexplainable joy, a joy that came with her full acceptance of her love for him, of her blind trust in him. She loved Alan no matter what he might have done. She trusted him and knew without any shadow of doubt that he wouldn't do anything to hurt her. She was too choked up on joy to answer him.

Alan couldn't read her face because she brought her hands up to her flushed cheeks and wiped the tears from her eyes. So he waited, not patiently, but he waited. He could imagine what an innocent man felt like, a man who was facing a maximum sentence for a crime he didn't commit.

His breath seemed constricted somewhere in the lower expanse of his chest, and he felt as if he were suffocating. He wanted to move, but he didn't. His green eyes, dull with pain, open for Megan's perusal, revealed the depth of his anxiety. He stared at the woman in front of him.

He was desperate for her love, but he hid his desperation, squaring his shoulders. Slowly, attempting to be nonchalant, he unbuttoned his shirt. He was afraid for her to answer, but this, too, he hid. One button, two, three . . . He wished she would speak.

Megan saw his soul, knowing and understanding. Her voice was strangely soft and gentle when she finally said, "Whether I believed her or not is of no consequence, my darling. What really counts is that I love you." She made the first step; she must reassure him. She must let him know how much she loved him. "For all time, Farmer McDonald, I love you." She smiled. "Remember, I am yours and you are mine."

She wrapped her arms around him, laying her head on his chest, wanting to feel the warmth and security of his arms around her. She did so, not knowing that he exercised infinite control to keep from squeezing her too tightly. He murmured her name over and over, love thickly coating each murmur.

Her name had never sounded so lovely. "I don't care, Alan," she declared in an emotionally hoarse voice. "I don't care if you did marry me for the hacienda. I love you, and if you want the Hacienda del Lago Lindo, then that's what I want."

He cradled her tightly to his chest, and she listened to the booming of his heart as his hand ran over the back of her head down the shining strands of her hair.

"The hacienda is the least of my wants." His hands slid to her upper arms, clasping them, setting her slightly in front of himself. Earnestly the green eyes, solemn and filled with the wonder of love, peered into her soft gray ones. "My greatest desire is to make you happy because I love you, Megan."

"I love you," she whispered, her eyes shimmering with tears, never tiring of saying the words to Alan, never tiring of hearing Alan say the words to her.

"I'm only sorry that I didn't take the time to discuss Linda with you." She saw the frown of concern on his brow; she felt the shrug of his shoulders. "I never dreamed that Elena would use it to hurt you." His eyes searched hers, flicking over her entire face, coming to rest on those glowing eyes that mirrored the happiness of her soul. "I didn't want the property badly enough to sacrifice my freedom a second time in a loveless marriage, nor do I want it badly enough to sacrifice my marriage of love for it."

"But," Megan gently reminded him, "you were caught up in the building of the hacienda. Look at all the research that you and Ric had already done. And," she pointed out,

180

"those sketches weren't done in the past three or four weeks."

Suddenly the weariness of the day and the anxiety of the past few hours pressed upon him. He turned her loose, flexed his arms, and walked around the bedroom.

"I wanted to rebuild the hacienda," he confessed, "and I intended to get the property if I could." He smiled mischievously. "At the time, though, I didn't know that I'd get you to boot." His eyes shined with love. "When Ric and I were doing the research and making the sketches, we didn't know if our hacienda would become a reality or not. Then, that day at the lake, I knew that you and I had this one thing in common. Our goal was the same. Both of us wanted to build the hacienda."

"And," Megan continued softly, pointing an accusing finger, "you did have a dream. You won't admit it, and you disguise it under the cloak of a goal, but it was a dream."

Again he chuckled. "If building the hacienda is to fulfill anyone's dream, Meggie," he averred, "it's to fulfill yours. You made me realize that this could become more than a few squiggles on a sheet of paper. I knew that you and I could make a home out of the hacienda. I knew that we could give Matt back part of his rich Mexican heritage."

"Yet you promised Linda that you would build the hacienda for her!" Megan could still see the small, beautiful signature in the left hand corner of the sketch. She could hear Alan's answer to her question.

Alan shook his head, and his eyes twinkled. "I told you that a yes or no answer was impossible, Megan. And it is. You asked me if I promised Linda that I would buy back all the Mateo y Mendoza property. I answered that question. You never asked me about the hacienda, and I never stated that I would build it for Linda."

"I saw the sketch," she argued. "Elena took the sketch out of the portfolio."

Alan grinned, and his eyes grew more amused. "You fell victim to an old trick, my darling wife." He paused then explained. "That happened to be one of the sketches for this house. Remember, I told you that Linda and I worked on the renovation of this one."

Megan stared at him, the truth dawning. Elena had snared her into believing what Elena wanted her to believe. Megan had been so upset that she didn't really look at the sketch. She only looked at what Elena pointed at: the signature and the date.

"Linda and I never discussed the hacienda until she was dying, and then it wasn't to plan the constructing of it. She was interested in my acquiring the property for Matt's birthright. I agreed with her," he continued. "I also wanted the property intact for Matt. I think it's a wonderful heritage for him."

Megan nodded, agreeing with Alan, relief surging through her body. "Elena lied about all of it," she said, looking into his face for verification.

"No," he slowly denied with a shake of his head. "She didn't exactly lie about all of it. She just doesn't know the full truth."

"But," Megan contended, frowning in puzzlement, "I don't understand."

"She's exaggerated for the most part," Alan explained, "and she's repeated what she's heard Rosa and Mother talk about." He frowned. "I didn't know Elena could be so cruelly vindictive, but she told you the truth as she saw it." Now he smiled, that smile which was reserved only for Megan. "Trouble is, she didn't see too clearly. Everyone," he went on, "including Rosa and Mother, believed that I buried myself out here with Linda's memory, but I didn't. I enjoy living here; I enjoy being a simple dairy farmer; and I like the people." Again he smiled, glad to have penetrated that wall of doubt and uncertainty that Elena had ably helped Megan erect.

Then Megan asked another question, not out of jealousy or because of doubt. The answer wouldn't diminish her joy. She simply wanted to satisfy her curiosity. "Were you planning to live with Linda again when she returned?"

He shook his head yet another time and completely unbuttoned his shirt, letting it fall apart in the middle to hang loosely from his jeans. "I wouldn't have lived with Linda again, period." Megan's smile pleased him. "But Elena is right." He saw Megan's brows furrow with puzzled question. "I did spend the last two weeks of Linda's life with her."

Megan could see him retreat to his memories, and she felt the sadness that encompassed him. He paused for a minute, then he spoke.

"When I arrived the doctors told me that she had no chance."

"Did she know?" Megan asked.

He nodded. "The doctors hadn't told her, but she knew. And like so many people who know that they're dying," he said, pushing his shirt back on each side and clasping his hands to his hips, "Linda began to regret many decisions in her life. She was suddenly repentant. She wanted to restore the Mateo y Mendoza land grant for Matt; she wanted to become a mother to him; she wanted to become the wife to me that she'd never been."

"Why was Linda coming home?" Megan asked. "What made her think she'd be welcome?"

He dropped his hands and walked to the bed, flipping back the bedspread before sitting down. "Linda was in her first starring role, and she was drumming up all the publicity that she could. She and her agent decided that the domestic touch would help. She called and wanted me to bring Matt to the set, so she could have some photos made with him, but I refused. She threatened to come to the farm, but I didn't believe her."

He sat on the edge of the bed and began taking off his

boots and socks. "She carried out her promise. She and the guy she was living with were on their way to get Matt when they were in the car accident."

"You never told Rosa and Elena this?" Megan quietly murmured. "All these years you've let them believe that Linda was really coming home."

"There was no need to tell them differently," he stated, throwing his socks on the floor with his boots. "Knowing that she was coming home made it easier for them to accept her death, and it made no difference to me either way."

"Did you—did you still love her?" Megan crossed her arms over her chest as if she were shielding herself from his answer.

"I still loved her," he admitted gently, and Megan flinched from the hurt that shot through her heart like an arrow. He saw the pained expression on her face and he explained, "Love is an emotion that you can't turn off and on like a spigot, Megan." He moved to the window, gazing vacuously at the empty lawn below, one hand resting on his hip, the other on the casement. "When the love is one-sided like mine was, I wished it were different. I wished I didn't love her, but I did." The he turned, his shirttail swishing against his legs, the muted light glistening on his bare chest. "I wouldn't have taken her back though." His voice softened. "I never went after her once, Megan. I never ran after her."

He hoped and prayed that Megan understood. He wanted her to understand that it was possible to love more than once. He wanted her to understand that his love for Linda didn't take away from the magnitude of his love for her. He loved each differently; he loved Megan more completely, more fully.

"And you told her that you loved her?" Megan quietly asked, Elena's accusations still harshly ringing in her mind.

She saw the tightening of his mouth; she saw the furrows in his brow; she saw the censure in his green eyes. But she wanted one last assurance.

"Will I have to go through life convincing you over and over again that I love you, that you mean more to me than Linda?"

"No," Megan answered, "but I would like you to explain just this once."

He rocked back and forth from heel to toe, eventually saying, "Yes, Elena was right. I did tell Linda that I loved her, and if I had it to do over again I would say the same words again." He stared at her a full second before he continued to speak. "Linda was so fuzzy from all the medicine that she was given that she was living more in the past than in the present. Mostly she remembered our first year, and we relived all our happier moments. Sometimes we would talk about Matt." He paused again. "I'm not sure if she remembered Matt or if she remembered only what I told her about him." Megan saw his eyes darken with sadness. "Each time she awoke she wondered where she was, and I'd go through the same routine again, saying the same thing over again. Over and over again," he said, his voice heavy, "until she died."

"Elena didn't bother to tell me that," Megan muttered, a sad smile playing around her mouth, needing no more explanation, wanting no more. She walked to the window to stand beside Alan and put her arm around his waist.

"Do you understand now" he asked, his arm sliding around her shoulders, his fingers squeezing her upper arm. He leaned his head, resting his cheek against the silken thickness of her hair.

She nodded. "Yes." No equivocation, no doubt.

"A one-sided love is never rewarding or fulfilling. Always there is that feeling of emptiness." Then she heard the soft, husky words, and his grip tightened on her arm. "I never knew the beauty of being loved until I met you.

185

You've filled all those vacancies and voids. You've made me a complete man."

"And you've made me a complete woman," she murmured, turning in his arms, nestling her face as close to the warmth of his chest as possible.

Only one more misunderstanding to explain, he thought, loving the feel of her softness in his arms, deeply inhaling the light perfume which wafted from her body. He gently swayed her from side to side.

"Your grandfather called me." Megan nodded. "He called to let me know that he's coming home tomorrow."

Megan grinned. "Was he surprised to find out that we were married?"

Alan chuckled, his cheek still resting on the crown of Megan's head. "He was. He couldn't imagine our knowing each other, much less being married. Said he wasn't going away again. Too much happens when he's away."

Megan laughed softly with him. "Of course, I don't believe him. He won't be home a week before he'll be on the road again." She sighed, opening her eyes, looking at the silvery rays of moonlight that spilled on the lawn. "Now I have a confession to make." Her cheeks dimpled, and her smile widened, her eyes dancing with love. "I want you to know this, Alan McDonald." Her voice, however, was solemnly serious. "I wouldn't have run away. I'm no coward, and I fight for what I want, and I want you." She looked directly into his face. "I was determined to make you love me if you didn't. I was going to give Linda's ghost and Elena's memory a run for the money."

"There's never been a ghost in the running."

Megan pulled out of his arms, her hands sliding down the sinewy strength of each, coming to rest on his wrists. She gazed at him momentarily before she moved away. She lowered the blinds, drew the drapes, and turned, walking toward the bathroom. As she moved she unbuttoned her shirt.

"I know that now, but I didn't before."

Unlike Alan, who always hung his clothes up or dropped them in the clothes hamper, Megan let hers lie where they fell. Alan, still standing by the window, watched. He wondered what she would do next. The corners of his eyes crinkled with amusement as his lips curved upward. His eyes were once again that warm spring green that frolicked with merriment.

"What are you going to do now?" Indolently he followed her, picking up each piece of clothing that she discarded.

She turned, facing him, standing proudly tall, her jeans at her feet, garbed in nothing but her underwear. Her hands went to her back and unclasped her bra. She smiled, her eyes audaciously bold and daring, her smile coming from the deepest part of her inner being. Her hands closed over the narrow straps. She pulled them down, letting the bra fall to the floor at the same time that her breasts, crowned with darkened nipples, tingled into tightness and life.

Alan's eyes fastened on the satiny beauty, his groin suddenly taut and aching with an awareness of their full potential and promise. He stood transfixed, watching her fingers in one caressive movement sweep from her breasts down her midriff over her stomach to stretch the panty elastic to slip the lacy material over her thighs down her calves to the floor. She straightened, stepping out of the frothy material.

"I'm going to take a shower," she announced, spinning around, lifting her arms, the soft roundness of her buttocks flexing as she stretched her long legs. She glided gracefully into the bathroom, turned on the shower, and peeped around the door.

"You're not undressed yet?" she coyly asked with a tempting glint in her eyes, amorous fires burning low in their depths.

"Am I invited?" he asked, shedding his jeans and briefs in record time, moving into the bathroom at almost the same moment that he asked the question.

Megan's cheeks dimpled and she smiled, nodding her head. With coquettish movements meant to torment and titillate his senses, she lifted her arms again, her hands catching hold of the shower-curtain rod. Lazily she leaned backward against the coolness of the pale blue tile. She watched his green eyes spew spicy gimlets of love all over her, and she delighted in the pleasurable sting. She adored and welcomed the sensual onslaught of emotions.

His thumb and index finger curved gently around the budded peak, gently swirling around and around. Megan's eyes glazed with erotic hunger, and her body moved languidly with his rhythm. The closer he came; the closer her breasts swayed to the burning heat of his naked torso. She turned her face up to him, twining her arms around his shoulders, her hands locking on his neck.

Huskily came the whispered words. "I'm going to teach you all the intricacies of taking a shower with a woman."

Alan chuckled, stilling the movement of his fingers, his hands slipping under the weight of her breasts. She inhaled deeply and slowly, savoring the exotic touch. Her lips pouted for his kiss, coming nearer his face.

She couldn't resist the last teasing gibe. "Surely you're not embarrassed, Mr. McDonald!"

He loved the purring seduction in her words. "Not in the least, Mrs. McDonald." He shook his head, his face lowering by slow degrees, accentuating the delightful torment. "I'm just wondering if showering with you can be any more exciting than sleeping with you."

They both laughed together, drinking simultaneously of that sweet, rare vintage called love.

### LOOK FOR NEXT MONTH'S
### CANDLELIGHT ECSTASY ROMANCES ®

# Seize The Dawn

## by Vanessa Royall

For as long as she could remember, Elizabeth Rolfson knew that her destiny lay in America. She arrived in Chicago in 1885, the stunning heiress to a vast empire. As men of daring pressed westward, vying for the land, Elizabeth was swept into the savage struggle. Driven to learn the secret of her past, to find the one man who could still the restlessness of her heart, she would stand alone against the mighty to claim her proud birthright and grasp a dream of undying love.

A DELL BOOK    17788-X    $3.50

# Desert Hostage

## Diane Dunaway

Behind her is England and her first innocent encounter with love. Before her is a mysterious land of forbidding majesty. Kidnapped, swept across the deserts of Araby, Juliette Barclay sees her past vanish in the endless, shifting sands. Desperate and defiant, she seeks escape only to find harrowing danger, to discover her one hope in the arms of her captor, the Shiek of El Abadan. Fearless and proud, he alone can tame her. She alone can possess his soul. Between them lies the secret that will bind her to him forever, a woman possessed, a slave of love.

**A DELL BOOK      11963-4    $3.95**